SLUGS INVADE THE jam Factory

CHRISSIE SAINS

ILLUSTRATED BY
JENNY TAYLOR

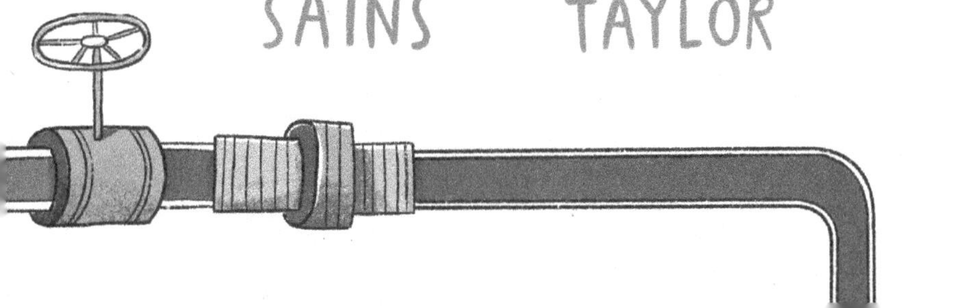

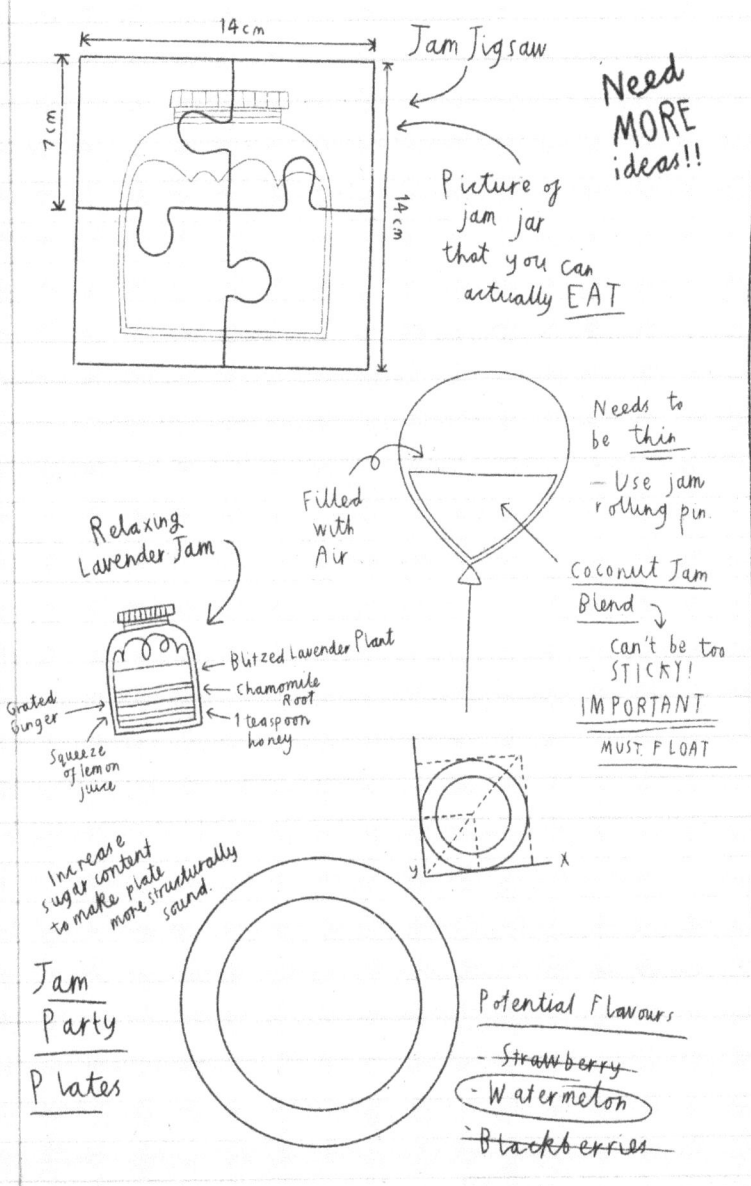

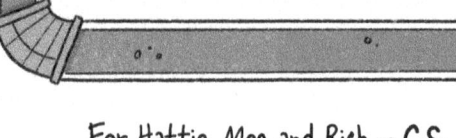

For Hattie, Meg and Rich – C.S.

To Granny and Popsy – J.T.

This is a work of fiction. Names, characters, places and incidents are either the product of the author's imagination or, if real, used fictitiously. All statements, activities, stunts, descriptions, information and material of any other kind contained herein are included for entertainment purposes only and should not be relied on for accuracy or replicated as they may result in injury.

First published 2023 by Walker Books Ltd
87 Vauxhall Walk, London SE11 5HJ

2 4 6 8 10 9 7 5 3

Text © 2023 Chrissie Sains
Illustrations © 2023 Jenny Taylor

The right of Chrissie Sains and Jenny Taylor to be identified as author and illustrator of this work has been asserted in accordance with the Copyright, Designs and Patents Act 1988

EU Authorized Representative: HackettFlynn Ltd, 36 Cloch Choirneal, Balrothery, Co. Dublin, K32 C942, Ireland. EU@walkerpublishinggroup.com

This book has been typeset in Stempel Schneidler

Printed and bound by CPI Group (UK) Ltd, Croydon CR0 4YY

All rights reserved. No part of this book may be reproduced, transmitted or stored in an information retrieval system in any form or by any means, graphic, electronic or mechanical, including photocopying, taping and recording, without prior written permission from the publisher.

British Library Cataloguing in Publication Data: a catalogue record for this book is available from the British Library

ISBN 978-1-5295-1068-3

www.walker.co.uk

CHAPTER ONE

Chief Inventor, Scooter McLay, stood outside the main entrance of McLay's jam factory. He looked from left to right, his eyes alert, his body tense. Slowly and carefully, he lay a plate of jam sandwiches on the ground. He searched the darkness outside, his gaze resting for a moment on a shadowy hawthorn bush to the side of the path.

Had something moved over there?

He watched a moment longer then shook his head. It was probably just a gust of wind.

He backed up into the safety of the factory, pressed the large, round *Door Lock* button and breathed a sigh of relief as the steel security door shut and the bolts clicked reassuringly into place.

"I really hope this plan works." He squinted out through a spyhole in the door as a jam tart hovered in the air by his shoulder.

"Me too, Scooter." A very tiny and very round alien peered over the pastry rim of the jam tart as she crossed her fingers nervously.

The alien was called Fizzbee.

Just like Scooter, Fizzbee was an inventor.

Just like Scooter, Fizzbee loved jam.

And she was orange … just like Scooter's hair.

Except Fizzbee was orange all over.

In fact, she looked a bit like a small orange ping-pong ball, but with two little arms and legs, two big eyes that took up half of her face and two antennae that she could use to make things fly. Most of the time she flew around in a jam tart beside Scooter's shoulder. Most importantly, Fizzbee was Scooter's best friend in all the world.

"It is … *quite* a good plan." She gave him a reassuring pat on the ear. "Fizzbee is … ummm … *sure* that it will work." She crossed both arms and legs, smiled sheepishly, then crossed her antennae.

"It won't." Scooter turned in surprise to see Daffy Dodgy leaning on the trunk of a banana tree behind him, studying her fingernails oh-so-casually.

"Believe me, those slippery little suckers are *organized*. That's why they always attack at night when the factory is closed." Daffy glanced at the letterbox, which was nailed shut, and gave the hammer in her pocket a sage pat. "Giving them a jam sandwich is just completely—"

"**Squeak**!" Daffy's pet guinea pig, Boris, finished her sentence with a roll of his eyes.

"Exactly, Boris!" Daffy agreed, her *Head of Security* badge gleaming proudly on her brown velour tracksuit. "I couldn't have said it better myself."

"**Squeak, squeak**." Boris glared witheringly at Scooter, before wriggling his bum uncomfortably in his hazmat suit.

This was the only way that Boris was allowed to enter the jam factory, following an incident involving an unidentified guinea pig poo found floating in the banana jam just last week. Boris and Daffy had sworn that it was absolutely nothing to do with them, but Scooter wasn't taking any chances when it came to factory hygiene.

Scooter turned back to the spyhole, his eyes locking on the plate of jam sandwiches outside.

There was no movement. No sound. Nothing.

What if Daffy was right? What if this plan wasn't going to work?

Except ... *it had to.*

Because – and this was a first for Scooter – *he was running out of ideas.*

He stood back from the door, turned towards his beloved factory and let out a long sigh.

When Scooter had decided to grow fruit and vegetables inside his jam factory, his only thought had been to make the jam as tasty as possible. After all, everyone knows that the best jam comes from the freshest fruit. But of course, in Scooter's typical way, he hadn't just grown some fruit.

Oh no.

Scooter had turned the entire factory into a tropical glasshouse. Or, as Scooter called it, a tropical jam-making paradise! And over the last few months, it had become so much *more* than that. Especially since Scooter's friend, Cat Pincher, had been helping them. Cat loved growing plants as much as Scooter and Fizzbee loved inventing jam. Under Cat's care, the plants had flourished and grown, and the tropical house was now bursting at the seams with all sorts of luscious, juicy, mouth-watering fruit.

Banana, coconut and even cocoa trees lined the walkways.

Scrumptious strawberry, raspberry and watermelon plants trailed along the walls.

Live Brussels sprout batteries powered giant robotic tools and machinery as they stretched and sliced, rolled and wrapped, sculpted and shaped jam into all of the various McLay's jam factory products. All to the hum, the drum and the thrum of the jam-making waterfalls and whirlpools as they chopped and churned, boiled and bubbled, swirled and, finally, supplied the most delicious jams *ever* made to the babbling brooks that meandered around the factory.

As far as Scooter was concerned, it was *perfect*.

A new planting area had been introduced for Cat. They'd installed a little

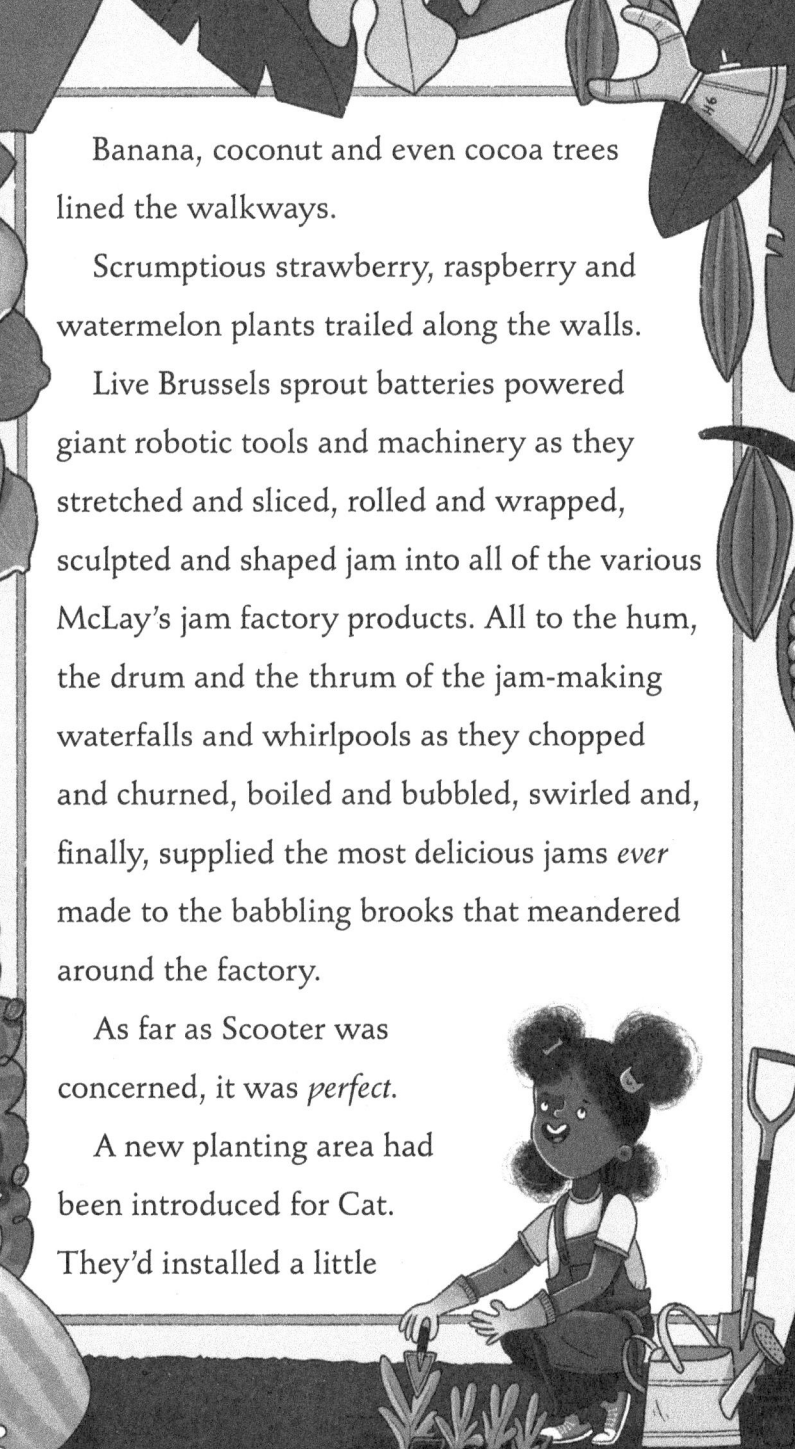

greenhouse, a potting shed, even a compost chute! And right beside it was Scooter and Fizzbee's testing area where they could work on their new jam inventions.

Watermelon Wonder Jam Party plates – use as a plate to hold a jam sandwich and some mini sausages (and maybe some cheese puffs), then crack it like toffee and eat it for your pudding.

Crackerjack Coconut Jam Balloons – experience the miracle of edible floating jam balloons!

Jam Jigsaws – put the jigsaw pieces together to create a picture of a jam jar you can actually eat!

Relaxing Lavender Jam – sit back and unwind with a dollop on your toast!

But there was a problem.

Apparently, Scooter, Fizzbee and Cat weren't the only ones who loved the tropical house. The dense air and lush vegetation had attracted a cold-blooded enemy…

SLUGS.

Every single day, Scooter, Fizzbee and Cat scoured the factory for traces of slug slime that led them straight to a fresh batch of slugs who had slithered their way inside. Somehow, despite the bulletproof glass, the alarm and the lasers, the slugs kept slinking in. They'd broken in through the vents, the letterbox, even the sewage pipes!

Scooter had to admit, as unlikely as Daffy's suggestion sounded, the slugs did seem a bit ... well *organized*. But that was impossible, wasn't it? Slugs weren't clever enough to be organized.

Were they?

Scooter glanced towards the New Inventions Testing Area, where some of his slug defence ideas were listed on a whiteboard.

SLUG DEFENCE PLAN

1. Ask them nicely not to break in any more. FAILED - Don't speak Slug!

2. Put Daffy and Boris on slug duty. FAILED - Daffy is TERRIFIED of slugs.

3. Give them a jam sandwich and make friends so they'll agree to stay outside.

He sighed. Scooter had never encountered a problem that he couldn't find a solution to. After all, he had a head full of ideas and inventions. They whizzed and whooshed, zipped and sparked around inside his brain with so much enthusiasm that Scooter's halo of bright orange hair stuck out from his head like the beams of a light bulb.

There was a reason for this.

It was all to do with the day that Scooter was born.

The day that newborn Scooter took eight whole minutes to take his first breath.

In those eight long minutes, as he hung between life and death, his brain had somehow developed *hyper-creativity*.

There were other side effects too.

Scooter had cerebral palsy, a condition which, for Scooter, meant that the muscles on the left side of his body were a little stiff and he had to wear an uncomfortable splint to stop his left foot from dragging. But that didn't worry Scooter. It made life a little harder sometimes, but it was a part of him, just like his dogged determination and his brilliant ideas.

Except, for a few weeks now, Scooter had noticed that his ideas felt less whizzy and whoossshy, less zippy and sparky and more … well, more of a … squidgedy *pffft*.

It was very odd. Not to mention inconvenient. It was the start of the school holidays and Scooter had planned to catch up with all of the jobs that needed doing around the factory. He had a to-do list as long as a bog

roll and now, with this whole slug problem, ideas were something that he could really do with *more* of, not *less*.

"Hey, Scoot!" Cat Pincher swung down from a rope bridge above his head. She was always swinging down from somewhere unexpectedly. "What's with the jam sandwich outside the front door?" She somersaulted off the rope bridge and landed on her mismatched socks and trainers beside him as Fizzbee circled her head gleefully.

"He's trying to make friends with the slugs." Daffy shook her head as she picked up Boris, popped him into a baby carrier on her front and joined them by the front door. "I mean, whoever made friends with a *slug*?" She shuddered.

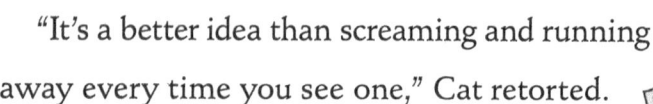

"It's a better idea than screaming and running away every time you see one," Cat retorted.

"Not much, though!" Daffy snapped. "I mean, Scooter's ideas haven't exactly been top notch recently." She glanced towards a wall covered in newspaper cuttings and awards that Scooter had received for his incredible jam flavours and inventions, then met Scooter's eyes. "Let's face it, they're not up to your usual standard." She shrugged before turning back to Cat. "And anyway, I do not scream and run away every time I see a slug!"

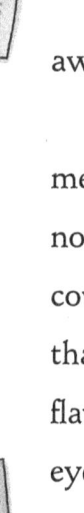

"Look!" Fizzbee squealed as she pointed through the spyhole. "The sandwiches, they have been nibbled! Scooter's plan is working!" Everyone crowded around for a peek. Fizzbee was right. The sandwiches had a couple of tiny bites taken out of them and the plate was covered in slug slime.

"Do you *really* think that means the plan's working?" Scooter stared at the plate suspiciously. "I wonder why they haven't eaten all of them."

"ARRRRRGGGGHHHHHHH!" Daffy began hopping from one foot to the other, her arms flapping overhead as three slugs dropped down from a pipe above on a string of slime. "Get away! Get away!" she wailed as she dived to the floor. "No, Scooter. I do *not* think the plan has worked!" she called over her shoulder as she crawled to the safety of a cocoa tree. "You need to come up with a proper plan next time. And that means one that's actually some GOOD!"

CHAPTER TWO

"But that was my last idea." Scooter's shoulders dropped as the spyhole in the door was covered by the unmistakable shape of a slug's bum and the letterbox began to rattle. He sank back into a conveniently located armchair right next to the front door and sighed as a stray hair flopped over his eyes. He brushed it out of the way angrily. Since when did his hair *flop*? What on earth was going on?

"Scooter?" Fizzbee hovered towards him as Cat cupped the slugs in an empty jam jar, opened the front door and flung them outside. "Is everything OK?"

"Yeah." Scooter shuffled in the armchair. "I just ... well, Daffy's right, isn't she? My ideas lately. They've been a bit rubbish."

Fizzbee, Cat and Daffy all met each other's eyes uncomfortably.

"You know, everyone has an off day sometimes, Scoot." Cat gave his shoulder a friendly rub as she sat next to him on the arm of the chair. "You'll probably wake up tomorrow with loads of ideas to stop the slugs."

"Yeah." Scooter nodded, even though he wasn't really sure about that. "Maybe."

"It sounds to me like you've got a bit of creative block." Daffy nodded sagely. "Us creatives all go through it at some point. I've been there myself."

"Really?" Scooter sat forwards in surprise. "How long did yours last for? And how did you fix it?"

"Well..." Daffy looked skyward, before taking a deep breath. "Mine's lasted just over seventy-eight years. And ... errrr ... I'm not sure how you fix it. I don't think I ever did."

"But Daffy, you're seventy-eight years old *now* aren't you?" Cat frowned.

"Seventy-eight and a *half*, actually." Daffy smoothed down her tracksuit top. "Not that I look it."

"Oh." Scooter slumped back. "Brilliant." He ignored the annoying rattling noise of the letterbox and turned towards two giant robotic hands that were extending down from the ceiling nearby. One was holding a pen, the other was clutching a rolled-up scroll.

"Hand-Bots?" Scooter called. "Please could you add *Unblock creativity* to my to-do list?"

Everyone watched as Hand-Bot Two unfurled the scroll with a flourish.

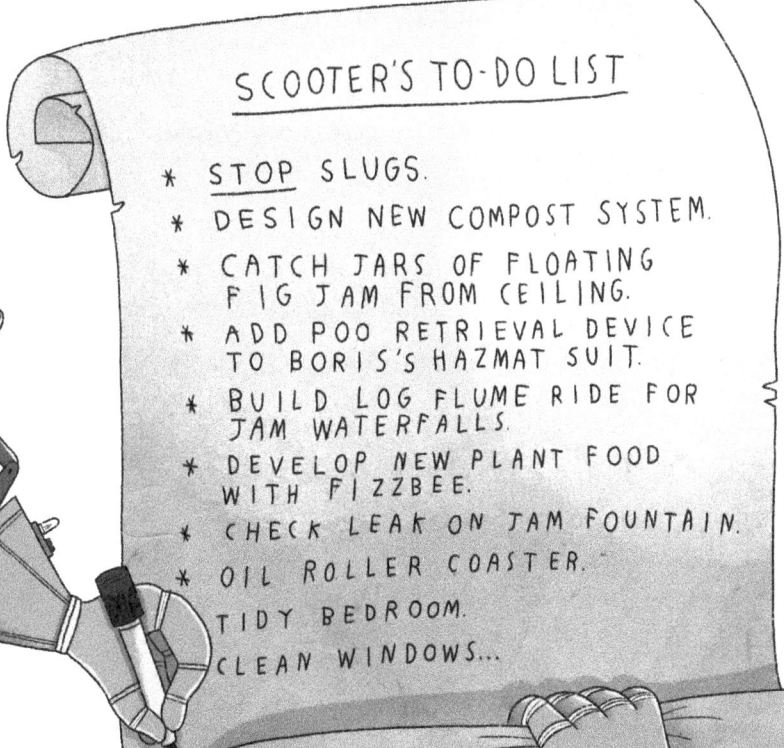

SCOOTER'S TO-DO LIST

* <u>STOP</u> SLUGS.
* DESIGN NEW COMPOST SYSTEM.
* CATCH JARS OF FLOATING FIG JAM FROM CEILING.
* ADD POO RETRIEVAL DEVICE TO BORIS'S HAZMAT SUIT.
* BUILD LOG FLUME RIDE FOR JAM WATERFALLS.
* DEVELOP NEW PLANT FOOD WITH FIZZBEE.
* CHECK LEAK ON JAM FOUNTAIN.
* OIL ROLLER COASTER.
  TIDY BEDROOM.
  CLEAN WINDOWS...

"Scooter, this list is enormous!" Fizzbee gasped as the scroll rolled down to the floor, then continued unfurling into the factory as Hand-Bot One chased it with a pen.

"No wonder your creativity has scarpered – that's far too much to think about! Nothing kills creativity quicker than a to-do list as long as that," Daffy declared wisely as she showed them her own to-do list scrawled on the back of her hand. "Personally, I try and keep mine as short as possible and I *still* have a creativity block."

TO DO
Security stuff.

"**Squeak**." Boris nodded in agreement.

"I hate to admit it, but I think Daffy's right." Cat stood up from the armchair, lifted Scooter's feet and rested them on a box. "Maybe you're having a bit of a block because you've got too many jobs to think about. Why don't you let us do some of them, then you'll have a bit less to think about? I bet you just need a rest. Why don't you take the afternoon off?"

"I'm not sure." Scooter frowned. He preferred to do certain jobs himself rather than getting help from other people. Nobody did things in quite the same way that he did. "It would be much easier if I could just do more." He sighed, watching as Fizzbee hovered her way down the to-do list, reading every item as she went. She stopped as Hand-Bot One wrote the words: *Unblock creativity.*

"Scooter?" She pulled a little piece of paper hesitantly out from her jam tart and drifted back towards him. "Fizzbee has been working on something that might help."

"Really, Fizz?" Scooter's heart soared. When Fizzbee first arrived at the jam factory, she'd brought a little suitcase of alien inventions with her that could do almost anything.

If Fizzbee had a solution, then Scooter felt sure that it would be something that could magically solve all his problems. "What is it?" He watched bright-eyed as Fizzbee opened the piece of paper and held it up in front of him.

Scooter stared at the recipe. It was the perfect solution! Not to mention that it sounded completely delicious. With Cocoa Bean Creativity Jam he'd be coming up with ideas again in no time! Then this whole slug problem would be easy to sort out.

"But, Scooter, it is a verrrrry complicated recipe." Fizzbee folded the piece of paper back up. "And it must incubate for one whole night first. It will be ready at dawn."

"Well, that won't be a problem." Scooter beamed. "We'll just have to keep the slugs out for one more day and then the Creativity Jam will unblock my creativity and I'll know *exactly* how to stop the slugs. In fact, I'll know how to fix *everything* on the list!"

"Do you really think that's the best solution, Scoot?" Cat bit her lip nervously. "You know how much I love Fizzbee's inventions, but maybe this isn't really a fix-it-with-jam kind of a problem? Maybe you just need a lovely Banana Jam bubble bath and a read of the latest *Jam Weekly* magazine?

You can relax and we can help you with your to-do list. I bet your mum and dad will help too if you speak to them about it."

"Well, if you ask me, all problems are a fix-it-with-jam kind of a problem." Daffy patted her perfectly coiffed hair. "Personally, I think Creativity Jam is a *brilliant* idea!"

"Squeak," Boris agreed.

Scooter hesitated. Cat had never warned him against making a jam invention before. And especially not when it came to using Fizzbee's inventions. Cat had been the first one to try Fizzbee's Floating Fig Jam and she hadn't hesitated when it came to using Fizzbee's Shrinking Strawberry Jam on their last adventure, either.

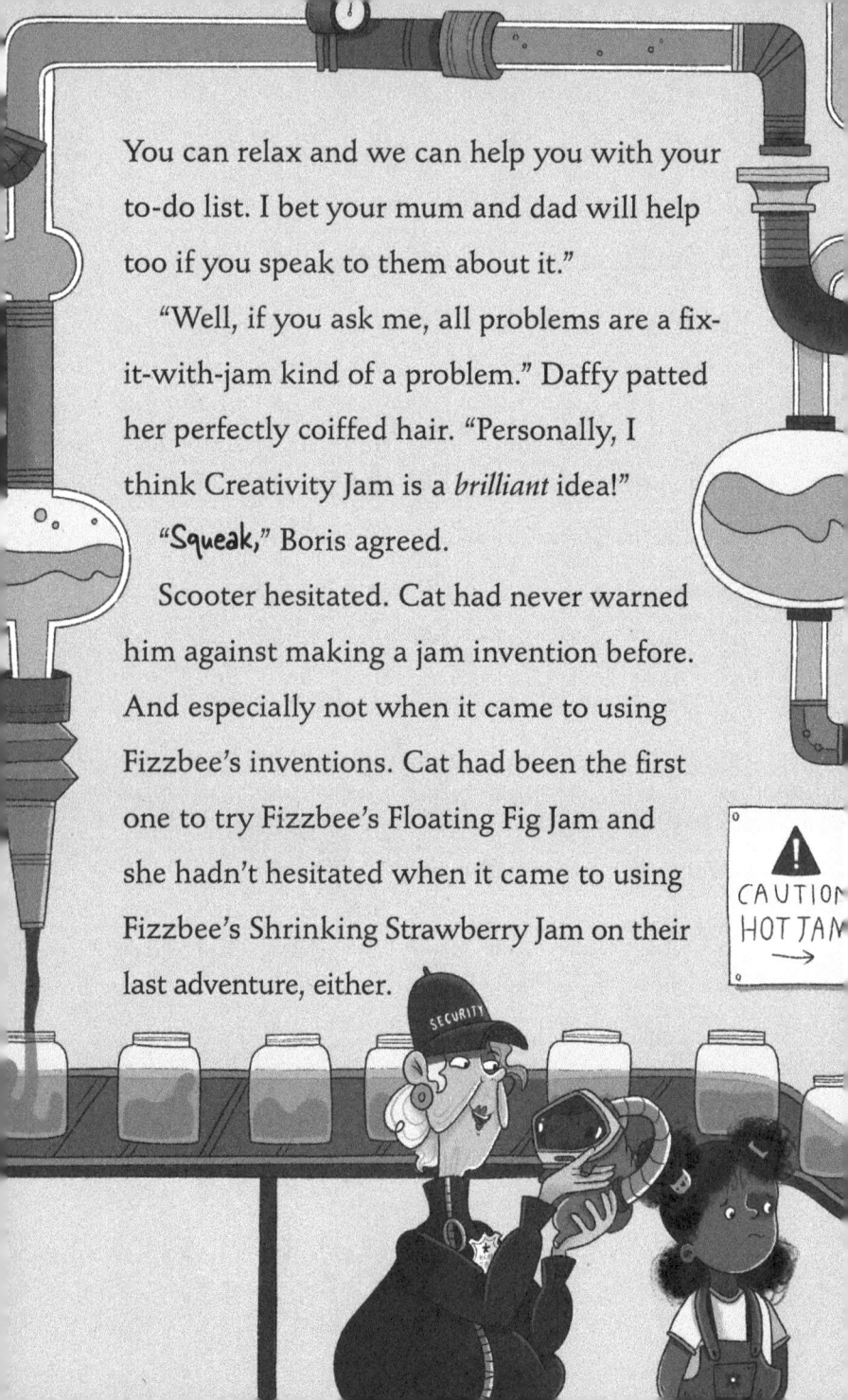

Plus, if Daffy thought it was a good idea, then that meant that it almost definitely *wasn't*. Scooter had to admit that Fizzbee's inventions didn't always go *quite* as they expected. Maybe it would be better to take Cat's advice and have a rest first. He glanced longingly at a little wooden rollercoaster cart sitting quietly beneath a track full of loops. It had been a while since he'd just had some fun.

"Cat's right." Scooter nodded. "Maybe I should just have a day off. And I should probably check with Mum and Dad about Cocoa Bean Creativity Jam. I guess if I'm not back to normal after a rest then we could—"

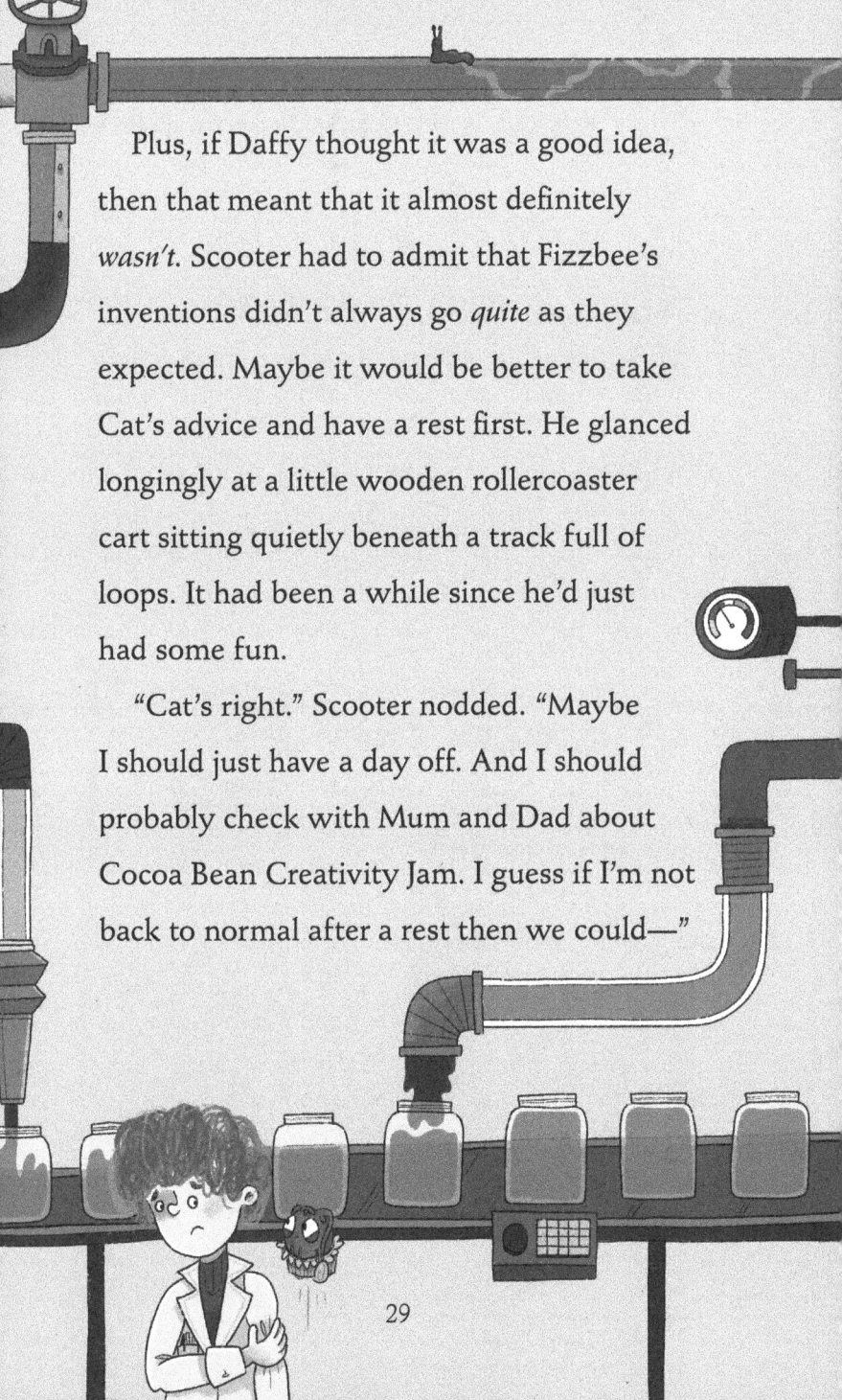

RATTLE, **BANG**, RATTLE, **BANG**, RATTLE, **BANG**.

Scooter turned slowly towards the letterbox. Why was it making that noise?

RATTLE, BANG, RATTLE ... **BANG, BANG, BANG ... FLUMP!**

He jumped as two ginormous slugs plopped out of the letterbox and onto the welcome mat, along with a very official-looking letter.

Cat popped the slugs into the jar again, then opened the front door and tossed them outside, as Scooter opened the letter.

Willowden Council

WILLOWDEN GREEN BRANCH

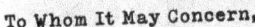

To Whom It May Concern,

I am writing to inform you that the annual hygiene inspection of McLay's jam factory will take place in two days.

Please note that if the following pests are found in your factory, it will result in an immediate fail and the factory will be closed down forthwith:

* snails
* slugs
* guinea pigs (unless properly attired)
* flamingos

I look forward to seeing you soon.

Yours faithfully,
Stanley Scrubs

Hygiene Inspector,
Willowden Green Branch

"Two days until a hygiene inspection?" Scooter looked up from the letter, his face draining of colour as Cat and Boris put all of their weight on the still-rattling letterbox to try and hold yet more slugs back.

"I told you they're organized." Daffy wailed as she backed away from the door.

"Well, this changes everything." Scooter pocketed the letter. "We'd better make the Cocoa Bean Creativity Jam first thing tomorrow morning!" He peered through the spyhole again as two tiny slug eyes peered right back at him. "We need to stop these slugs before the hygiene inspection and we don't have a moment to lose!"

CHAPTER THREE

Little did Scooter know that Daffy was in fact *right* and the slugs *were* organized.

Slugs are not normally organized.

While it's true that any slug would love to get inside McLay's jam factory and eat the delicious forbidden fruit that grew inside it, most slugs would probably just slither up a wall or a window, feeling around for an entrance until they realized it was easier to just eat something else.

Something like a plant pot, or an old wellington boot, or, better still, a rotten cabbage.

Slugs *love* rotten cabbages.

However, unfortunately for Scooter, Mucus Vane was not like most slugs.

OK, he might look like your average brown garden slug – though Mucus would argue that his slime was sleeker and his skin was smoother, and of course average garden slugs didn't have Mucus's snappy dress sense.

But Mucus was clever.

Not just clever for a slug. Oh no.

After all, a slug that can tell the difference between chocolate and poo would be considered a genius in the slug world.

No, Mucus would be considered clever in a room full of really clever *people*.

At least, he would if he could talk. Which obviously he couldn't. Being that he was a slug and most humans don't understand Slimeish (slug language), which is an intricate way of communicating via slug slime and looks like a complex sequence of bogey bubbles coming out of their bottoms.

For example, **Squelch squiiiiiiiisssshhhhhh** would mean, "I've found a great stash of food here!" in Slimeish. Or, **Gloooppppppy plooooopppppppy tfffhssshh** would be Mucus's answer if someone asked him the square root of pi (and he'd be right of course).

Mucus would rather that he didn't communicate via snot bubbles coming out of his backside. He'd prefer to be able to use human language. It seemed more sophisticated, if truth be told. But Mucus consoled himself that while he might not be able to talk like humans, he could definitely outwit them with

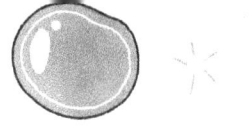
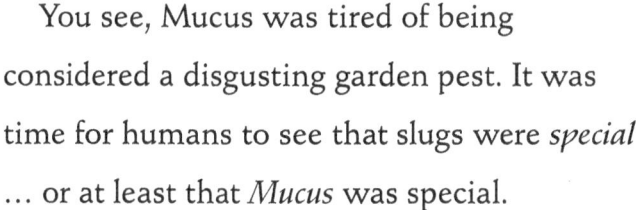

his superior brainpower.

You see, Mucus was tired of being considered a disgusting garden pest. It was time for humans to see that slugs were *special* ... or at least that *Mucus* was special.

It was Mucus who was devising all of the devious slug break-in plans.

And it was Mucus who was instructing and organizing all of the slugs. Not that it took much. After all, Mucus just needed to say, **Squelch squiiiiiiiisssshhhhhh** as loud as he could and the slugs would go wherever his slime trail led them. But all the same, no human could do that.

Mucus dreamed of turning McLay's jam factory into the first-ever slug café and wellness spa. A sanctuary for all the little slugs of the world, specializing in salt-free skin treatments. A place where humans would finally see what slugs were capable of.

Maybe one day in the future Mucus would even release a book about the glorious benefits of slug slime ... or at least a pamphlet.

He could picture it now: humans queuing up, *begging* for a glimpse inside the dazzling new complex (which of course would have a strict slug-only entry policy). They'd lavish him with gifts and awards and maybe even a crown for his incredible achievements. And, if he was lucky, they might even try to break inside and he would have the pleasure of throwing them out of the front door from a giant jam jar.

But first, he needed to take control of the jam factory.

And this was where Mucus's devious plans had hit a slight snag.

Finding new ways to get inside the factory was difficult enough, but *staying* inside? That was proving to be a big challenge. Mucus had been hurled out of the front door more times than he cared to admit.

But not for much longer.

Ever since Mucus had overheard Scooter and Fizzbee talking about Cocoa Bean Creativity Jam, he'd been determined to get some. It was the answer to all of his problems! After eating Cocoa Bean Creativity Jam, he'd know *exactly* how to take charge of the factory and, most importantly, how to keep the humans *out*!

It was for this reason that the next day, Mucus slimed his way slowly up the compost chute, past the mounds and mounds of rotten fruit and vegetables. Those daft humans never locked it, providing him with the perfect sneaky back route into the factory. As soon as he reached the top, he'd just need to hide until dawn. Then the jam would be ready and his for the taking.

Squarccccchhhhhhy squooooochy coooochy. He squelched past a mouldy strawberry, his excitement resembling a particularly effervescent bogey. **Squiddddgggggeedey ploop,** he giggled evilly.

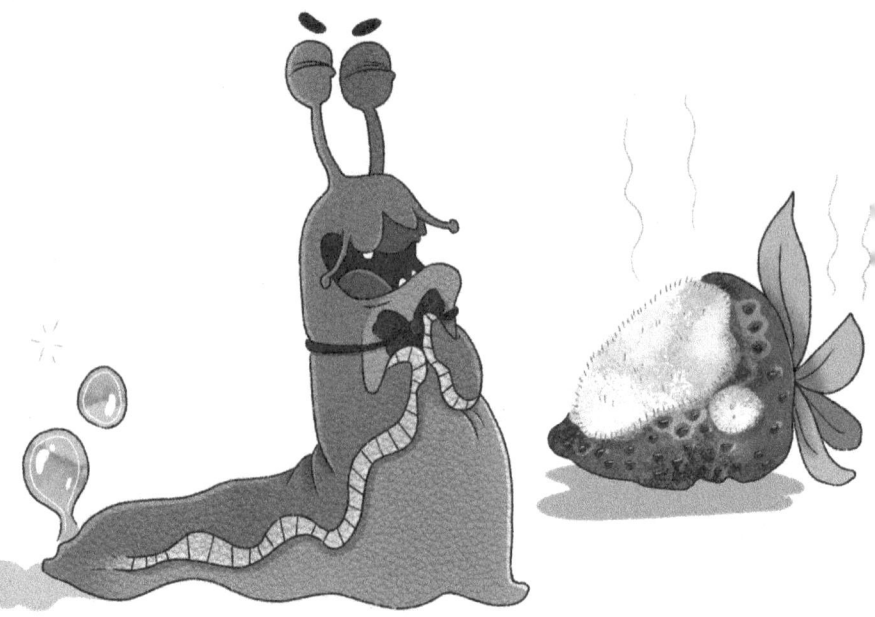

Back in the New Jam Inventions Testing Area, Scooter knew nothing of Mucus Vane and his dastardly plan. He was far too busy working with Fizzbee and Cat on a batch of Cocoa Bean Creativity Jam. He watched as Cat sliced open a cocoa pod, revealing a cocoon of tightly packed white seeds. She passed it to him and he emptied them into a large brass vat of bubbling jam.

McLAY'S JAM
JAM TESTING AREA

"Mmmmmmm." They all breathed in the most incredible smell of sweet, velvety chocolate as the vat fizzed and frothed.

"Well, it's definitely going to taste good." Cat picked up the empty cocoa pod and dropped it into the compost chute, before turning back to Scooter and Fizzbee with a nervous smile.

"And it will fix all of our problems." Scooter stared longingly inside the vat of bubbling jam. "So long as it works," he added.

"It will work, Scooter." Fizzbee opened her suitcase of inventions, then slowly and carefully pulled out a vial of dark brown sludge.

Liquid Fertilizer.

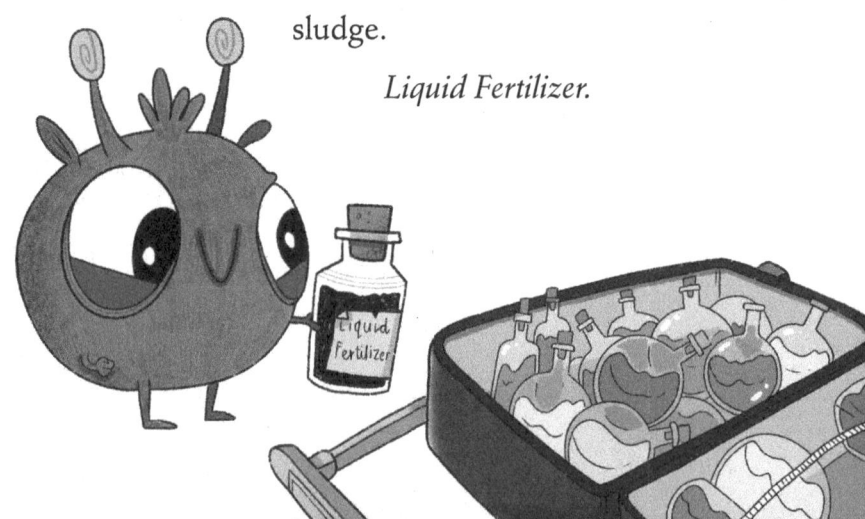

"But we must follow the recipe precisely." She squeezed the tiniest drop into the jam, which spat and sputtered for a moment, before turning a dark shade of brown.

"Errrr…" Scooter watched as Fizzbee took out what looked like a little pepper mill and added a generous twist over the jam. *Powdered Polyglot*. "Are you sure these are the right ingredients to make creativity?"

"Oh, yes, Scooter." Fizzbee took out one last jar from her suitcase: *Confidence Pulp*. She opened it carefully, took out a small spoonful, then emptied the rest of the jar into the brass vat. There was a satisfying crackle as the vat bubbled and bobbled, then burst into a cloud of the most delicious-smelling smoke.

Fizzbee gave a satisfied nod, put the spoonful back in the jar, closed the lid and placed it carefully back into her suitcase of

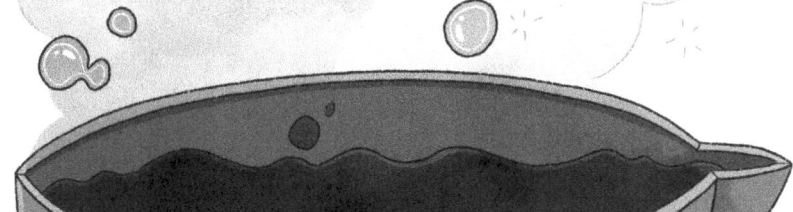

inventions. "Now, nobody must touch this while it incubates, Scooter. This is verrrry important. After all, we do not want too much creativity." She heaved her little suitcase onto her jam tart and lifted it towards a shelf behind them filled with books, plant pots, packets of seeds, garden tools and hundreds of jars of Scooter and Fizzbee's latest jam inventions.

"Ummm, Fizz?" Scooter watched as Fizzbee pushed her suitcase next to one of Cat's books.

"Why do we need to be so careful? I mean, would too much creativity really be so bad?"

"Of course!" Fizzbee looked up in surprise. "Too many ideas are just as bad as no ideas."

"Really?" Scooter replied sceptically. "But … too many ideas sounds like a good thing?"

"No, Scooter." Fizzbee stared at him as if he had said something really very silly indeed. "Too many ideas is not good. Millions of ideas fizzing in Scooter's head all at once? This makes it impossible to decide on *anything*! The ideas just grow and grow until the creativity is toxic and that is verrrrry dangerous." She shook her head seriously. "Scooter's head would explode!"

"Oh." Scooter gave the Cocoa Bean Creativity Jam a nervous glance.

"You know, maybe we should just read up a bit on slugs." Cat pulled the slug encyclopedia from the shelf. "There might be something in this book that will help stop them."

"We won't need to read up on slugs once the Creativity Jam does its work." Scooter dismissed the idea. "This time tomorrow, I'll know *exactly* how to stop them."

"I guess." Cat slid the book back onto the shelf. "So –" she waggled her eyebrows happily – "does that mean you've got the afternoon off now? Because you definitely deserve one and there's not much point trying to get through your to-do list before you've had the Creativity Jam, don't you think?"

"Oh, that's a great point!" Scooter grinned as his eyes drifted towards the little rollercoaster cart. "Does anyone fancy testing out the Drop of Doom?" He beamed. "And then I'll ask Mum and Dad if we could order some pizza and have a sleepover!"

"Yay!" Cat and Fizzbee both clapped their hands in delight.

And so, as Scooter, Fizzbee and Cat whizzed and whirred and whooshed and whooped their way around the factory, none of them noticed an ordinary-looking slug, who was in fact anything but ordinary, as he slithered and slimed and slunk his way into the factory.

Mucus curled himself into a ball under a handy empty cocoa bean pod and waited patiently until dawn when the jam would be ready. As the sun began to rise, he unrolled himself and stretched, then slowly snaked his way up to the top of the vat of Cocoa Bean Creativity Jam.

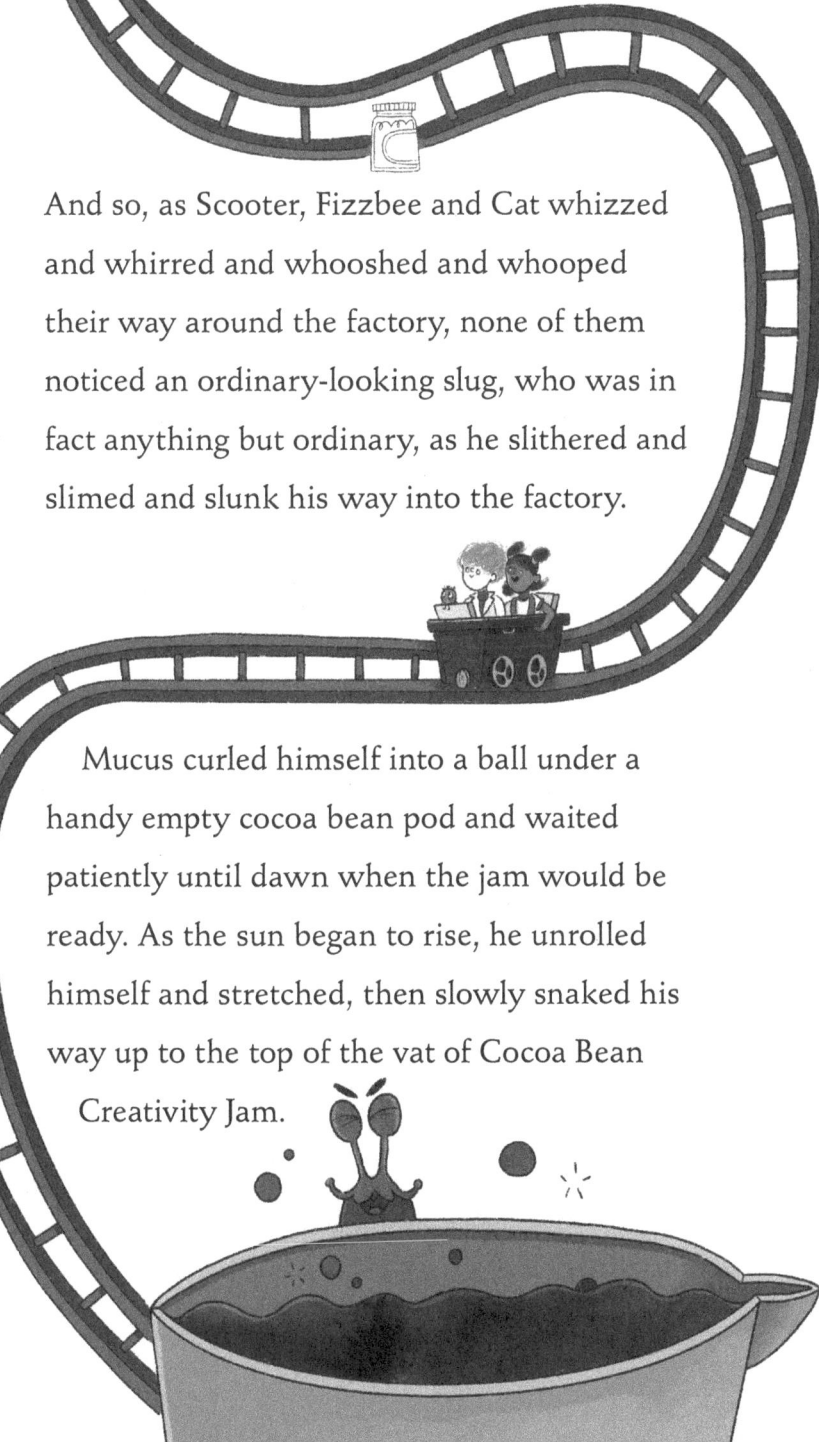

Squiddddgggggeey plop, Mucus cackled in glee as he peered over the edge of the bubbling vat and –

PLOP! –

he fell inside.

There was a bubble and a fizz and a spit and a whizz and then everything went dark.

CHAPTER FOUR

**SQUELCHHHHHHHHHH!
CRASSSSSSSHHHHHH!**

Scooter sat up in bed. What was that?

He looked at the clock.

4.42 a.m.

It was much too early for anyone to be up and about.

"Wazappening?" Cat looked up, bleary-eyed, from her blow-up bed on the floor.

"Aaaaaaaarrrrrgggggggghhhhhhhhhhh!"

A bloodcurdling scream rang out from the factory floor.

Scooter felt a jump in his hair where Fizzbee had been asleep.

"I'm not sure," he whispered as Fizzbee climbed down his ear and over to her jam tart on the bedside table. "But I think we should find out." He got up and struggled into his splint and dressing gown, then cautiously opened his bedroom door.

CREEAAAAKKKKK.

Scooter, Cat and Fizzbee poked their heads out.

"W-what's happened?" Dad yawned from outside the doorway.

"Yes. What was that noise?" Mum tied up her dressing gown and marched to the red front door of their little flat, a spanner held aloft.

They all peered over the banister towards the factory below.

The McLays lived in a small flat above the oldest part of the jam factory, which was made of two buildings. There was the tropical house, where Scooter spent most of his time and then there was the old factory, where Scooter lived upstairs with his parents and where McLay's jam factory had started out. Scooter travelled

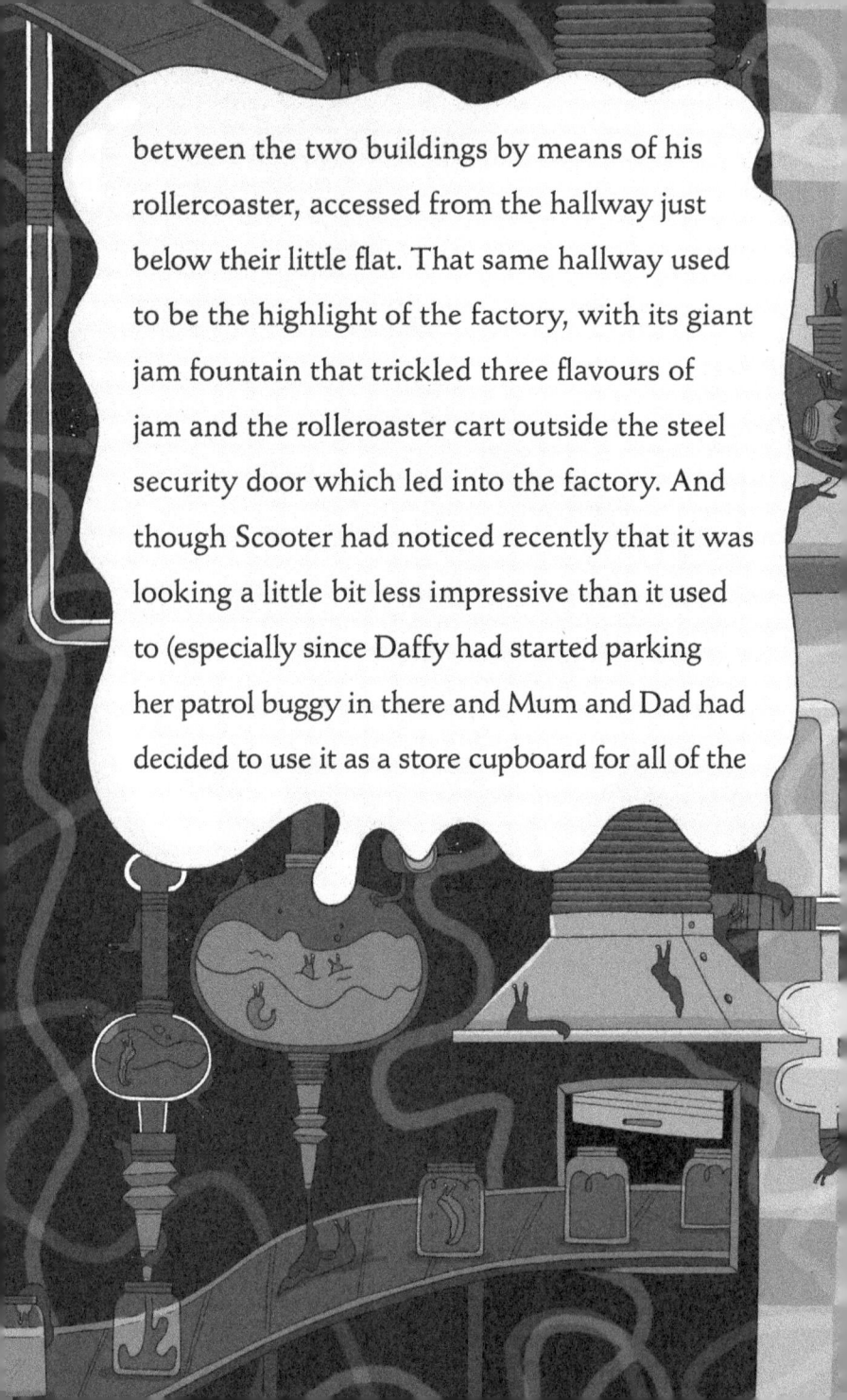

between the two buildings by means of his rollercoaster, accessed from the hallway just below their little flat. That same hallway used to be the highlight of the factory, with its giant jam fountain that trickled three flavours of jam and the rolleroaster cart outside the steel security door which led into the factory. And though Scooter had noticed recently that it was looking a little bit less impressive than it used to (especially since Daffy had started parking her patrol buggy in there and Mum and Dad had decided to use it as a store cupboard for all of the boxes of jams that weren't selling particularly well), he wasn't prepared for the sight that met his eyes as he peered over the banister.

There was slime *everywhere*.

Trails and trails of it covered the floor, the walls, even the ceiling! Fat drops of goo oozed over everything. The jam fountain was no longer trickling three flavours of jam. Instead, it *gloop*ed and *bloop*ed and *sloop*ed as at least a hundred slugs wriggled and writhed inside it.

"URGH!" Mum and Dad backed up towards the flat.

"It's a proper infestation!" Mum cried. "We've got to do something! Quickly!"

Scooter watched as they both legged it towards the kitchen, the little red door swinging shut behind them as he heard the words, "I'll grab some salt or maybe some egg sh..."

SQUELCH.

Scooter stared hard at the door. That wasn't your standard door-closing kind of noise. He gaped, then gasped as an army of slugs glued the door shut with their slime.

"SCOOTER? SCOOTER, WE CAN'T OPEN THE DOOR!"

RUUMMMBBBLLLLLEEEEE.

Scooter, Cat and Fizzbee turned slowly back towards the factory as they heard a faint rumbling noise.

"Where's the rollercoaster cart?" Scooter gripped the banister as he searched below. But the little cart was nowhere to be seen.

"Urgh!" He lifted his hand in disgust. It was covered in slime.

RUUMMMBBBLLLLLEEEEE.

"Scooter!" Fizzbee hovered protectively by his shoulder. "The noise, it is getting louder."

"And the doors." Cat sidled in towards them. "Are they starting to shake a bit?"

They all took a cautious step back.

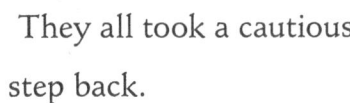

RUMMMMMMMMMMBB BBBBBLLLLLLEEEEEEEEEEE!

"SCCCOOOOOOO TTTTEEERRRRRRR!"

The steel security doors flung open and Daffy and Boris hurtled out of the factory on the tiny rollercoaster cart. It screeched to a sudden stop and then, strangest of all, Hand-Bots One and Two extended down from the ceiling, picked Daffy and Boris up and flung them unceremoniously out of the door. The hands dusted themselves down as the rollercoaster cart trundled back inside, then slammed the steel security doors closed.

""Daffy?" Scooter walked down the stairs towards them. He moved carefully, his right leg leading, taking one step at a time. All the gunky slime on the banisters made the steps a bit trickier than usual. "What's going on?"

"It's the slugs!" Daffy cried. "Scooter... *Slugs are invading the jam factory!*"

"Slugs are ... WHAT...?"

"Quickly! We've got to get out of here." Daffy sprinted towards her patrol buggy, launching herself and Boris inside. "The factory's finished." She shook her head. "All we can do now is save ourselves!"

"What do you mean 'the factory's finished'? And anyway, we can't just leave. My mum and dad are still in the flat!"

"I'm sorry, Scooter, but it's every man for themselves now." Daffy began fiddling frantically with the controls. "That's probably the safest place for them! The slugs have taken over all of your machinery. We've got to get out of here! Who knows what they'll do next!"

The steel security doors opened once again and a giant rolling pin began trundling menacingly towards them.

"How is it even doing that?" Scooter struggled to make sense of what was happening. "Who's in charge? And how could they...?" He stopped talking as the giant rolling pin halted and Hand-Bot One rose up slowly behind it, a little brown slug in its palm.

A little brown slug with rather snappy dress sense.

"Ahem," Mucus Vane cleared his throat importantly. "I think you'll find that I'm in charge now." He spoke in a posh, nasal voice.

"What?" Scooter's mouth fell open. "But ... I ... but ... how...?"

"Actually –" Mucus looked directly at Fizzbee before turning back towards Scooter –

"you've got your little friend to thank for that. The Cocoa Bean Creativity Jam worked a treat." He smirked. "Thanks ever so much."

Fizzbee's antennae shrunk back in surprise. "Fizzbee's recipe? Did this?" She glanced anxiously over her shoulder towards Scooter, then back to Mucus, her eyes lowered. "It does not matter how much creativity you have –" she spoke quietly, her fists clenched – "because Scooter still has more! Scooter is the greatest jam inventor in the world!" She lifted her fist angrily. "And this is Scooter's factory! He will stop you!" She zipped towards the rolling pin and gave it an angry kick.

"Yeah!" Cat put her arm around Scooter. "You're just a slug! You don't

seriously think you can outsmart Scooter McLay, do you?"

"Ummm..." Daffy watched from the patrol buggy. "Am I the only one here who's wondering how the slug is TALKING?"

"Just a slug!" Mucus roared before anyone had a chance to answer. "You wait and see what *just a slug* can do!"

"I think you might have annoyed him!" Daffy revved the engine of the little patrol buggy as Boris nervously deposited a little poo pellet into his hazmat suit. "Time to go!"

"And for starters –" Mucus lifted a remote control with his sensory tentacles and pressed a button – "this is no longer a jam factory. It is now the world's first slug café and wellness spa!" He lifted a megaphone to his slimy backside and,

SQUELCH SQUIIIIIIISSSSHHHHHH!

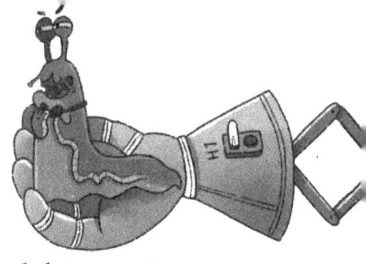

A huge squishing, sliming, belching noise erupted out of the megaphone.

"I've invited all of my fellow slugs to join me here." Mucus pressed another button on the remote control and the enormous rolling pin began lurching across the floor once again, squishing boxes of old jam in its wake. "It's time for you to leave now. Goodbye." **Squiddddggggeedey ploop**. Mucus let out an evil slimy giggle.

The steel security door swung shut, leaving Scooter with one last glimpse of the devilish twinkle in Mucus's eyes before the giant rolling pin began to pick up speed threateningly towards them.

"Quickly, everyone, onto the patrol buggy!" Scooter bellowed as the team piled in, while he followed as quickly as he could behind them. Everyone waited as he clambered into the buggy, then with one last glance up towards the flat, they zipped out through the front door just as the slugs slimed it shut behind them. At least Mum and Dad would be safe inside. "We need to get over to the main entrance!" Scooter shouted. "If we can just get to my inventions, then maybe it's not too late to stop the slugs!"

Daffy gripped the steering wheel and the buggy bolted towards the main entrance, screeching to a halt as they neared it.

"No!" Scooter cried, his face draining of colour at the sight ahead.

The Hand-Bots were flinging things out of the factory window. Broken parts of machinery, the whiteboard, books, even Cat's little potting shed! Scooter ducked as his beloved jam inventions book zipped past his ear and landed in a puddle, right next to a line of slugs that reached as far as the eye could see.

"Scooter, what are we going to do now?"

Cat gasped as they watched the hundreds – no, *thousands* – of hungry slugs slithering their way into the factory through a tiny slug-sized entryway at the bottom of the factory door.

"I…" Scooter hesitated. "I…"

"It is OK, Scooter." Fizzbee picked up his inventions book and handed it to him. "Whatever your plan is, we will all help you."

Scooter looked at the book in his hand as they all waited patiently for him to tell them what to do.

"I don't like to rush you." Daffy looked at her watch, then back at the long line of slugs. "But if there was ever a time that we needed your ideas, then it's right now!"

"I know." Scooter shook his head. "But…" His halo of orange hair fell flat around his head. "I'm sorry." He slumped. "I don't have any."

"Say, 'Aaaaaah'." Cat looked inside Scooter's mouth as they all squeezed into the little potting shed, which by sheer luck had landed the right way up when it was chucked out of the window.

"Aaaaahhh." Scooter held his mouth open.

"Hmmmm." Cat stood back and raised a pen in front of him. "Can you follow this pen with your eyes as I move it?" Scooter watched the pen as Cat moved it from left to right, then up then down, then round and round in a circle.

"Riiiiiiggggghhhhht." Cat tucked the pen down her sock. "Yeah. I can't see anything obvious." She shrugged as Fizzbee hovered in front of Scooter in her jam tart, her chin resting in her hand as if pondering a very difficult maths problem.

"This is verrrrry strange, Scooter." Fizzbee peered closely at his head, then lifted a stray strand of his hair, her brow furrowing as it flopped down. "But it is true." She landed her jam tart on Scooter's shoulder and turned to face everyone, her hands on her hips. "Scooter is having no ideas."

"What? None?" Daffy lifted her hands in despair.

"Nope." Fizzbee shook her head matter-of-factly. "Not one. Nil. Nada. Zero. Zilch. If this room was full of ideas, not one of them would be coming from Scooter."

"Literally *none*?" Scooter tried to hide his dismay. Fizzbee could see ideas like bubbles of colour around a person's head. If she said that he had none, then there was no doubt about it. But it was Scooter's ideas that had brought Fizzbee to Earth – she'd been able to see the colours of his creativity all the way from space! Had all of that creativity just disappeared like a puff of smoke?

"Well, I must say, that's *very* unhelpful." Daffy glared at Scooter. "This isn't a good time for your creativity to go on strike! We *need* it." She crossed her arms, then turned towards Fizzbee. "There's only one thing for it. You're going to have to whip up some more of that Cocoa Bean Creativity Jam. Fight fire with fire and all that." She clapped her hands as Fizzbee hesitated. "Well, what are you waiting for? Chop-chop. We need Scooter's ideas back right now! Off you go!"

"Ummm." Fizzbee gulped. "Fizzbee cannot make more Cocoa Bean Creativity Jam. Fizzbee only had enough ingredients to make one batch. And Fizzbee's suitcase is in the factory, so ummm..."

"The factory! Of course!" Cat hit her forehead. "Where there's more Creativity Jam! Maybe if one of us could break into the factory and get it, then we could fix Scooter and sort out those slugs! Maybe I could..."

"No." Fizzbee shook her head again. "If the Cocoa

Bean Creativity Jam has been contaminated by slugs, it is not safe for Scooter to eat."

"Oh." Daffy slumped down on an upturned plant pot with a roll of her eyes. "Well, that's just *great*."

Scooter sighed as he sat down wearily next to her. He had to agree. He'd thought having a little less creativity was bad enough but having *none*? That was a total disaster! And now, the very invention they'd made to fix the problem had actually created a much bigger problem. The factory had been taken over by an evil slug, Scooter had no idea how to fix it and they had a hygiene inspection in *two* days! He swiped a stray hair out of his eyes as he peered through the window towards the line of slugs slithering into the factory. There was no way that they'd pass right now! And if they couldn't pass the hygiene inspection, then the whole factory would be closed down!

But that wasn't what worried Scooter most of all.

There was one problem that Scooter could barely allow himself to think about because every time he let the thought into his mind, his heartbeat quickened, and his stomach clenched and he had to concentrate very hard on breathing.

What if he never had any ideas again?

"So?" Cat interrupted his thoughts. "What do we do now?"

"Ummm." Scooter didn't have an answer. He shrugged as Cat sighed and started picking up the books from the floor, stacking them in a

neat pile. She picked up the slug encyclopedia, gave it a thoughtful look, then sat on the pile of books and started flicking through it.

"I knew that jam was a bad idea." Daffy muttered. "I said so, didn't I, Boris?"

"**Squeak**." Boris nodded and they both gave Fizzbee a frosty glare.

"Well..." Scooter took a deep breath. "There's nothing we can do about unblocking my creativity right now. We're just going to have to find a way to stop the slugs and get the factory back *without* any good ideas from me." He stood up, relieved for a moment that although his creativity may have deserted him, his determination still seemed very much intact. "Fizzbee, how long do you think the Cocoa Bean Creativity Jam will last on the slug?"

"Maybe one day?" Fizzbee held up one finger.

"Oh, really?" Scooter brightened. "Well, that's not so—"

"Or one year?" Fizzbee spread her arms wide, before giving everyone a sheepish smile.

"Fizzbee does not really know." She grimaced. "The calculations were for a human, not a slug."

"Oh." Scooter rubbed his forehead as he thought it over. "If we could just get control of the Hand-Bots again," he mused. *"Then* maybe we'd have a chance." He paused as he remembered the remote control that the slug had been holding, then turned to face everyone, his jaw set in a grim line of determination. "We need to get those slugs out of *our* factory. If we can get inside and take the remote control, then just maybe we can find a way. Didn't you say something about breaking in, Cat?"

"Oooh, yes." Cat looked up from the slug encyclopedia brightly. "That evil slug wouldn't have a hope of keeping us out if he didn't have control of the Hand-Bots. And when it comes to getting all of the slugs out of the factory, I think this book might give us some ideas." She gave the book a pat. "With a bit more reading anyway."

"Great." Scooter picked up his jam inventions book from the floor, smiling as it fell open to a blank page. It was time for him to do something that he had never needed to do before.

"Let's have a team brainstorm." He nodded firmly. "We need to break into the factory and get that remote control. Ready? I want to hear *all* of *your* ideas."

Mucus Vane sat on a sun-lounger beside a luxurious bath full of Banana Jam bubble bath, sipping a rotten cabbage juice from a posh glass through a curly straw.

Everything had gone perfectly.

He'd known just what to do as soon as his smooth little body had hit the Cocoa Bean Creativity Jam. Take control of the giant

robotic hands and tools and then he would have absolute jam factory domination!

By the time he'd slithered his way out of the vat of jam, like a butterfly emerging from its chrysalis, he'd known exactly how to do it too. With just a few tweaks to the wiring and a brand-new remote control, the slugs would be in and the humans would be out. As soon as he was inside and, most importantly, in control, it had been the work of a moment to turn the jam factory into the world's first (and best) slug café and wellness spa.

He'd started with the warm jam brooks and streams, turning them into fancy new slug swimming pools. Happy little slugs could sit under the waterfalls as warm jam rained luxuriously down on them, before they took a dip in the bubbly slug jacuzzi.

Next, he'd reprogrammed the giant paintbrushes to provide a lovely gentle slug massage.

The area of the factory where Jam Wrapping Paper was made had been adjusted to give a wonderful hydrating jam body wrap.

The sweet moulds were now private slug slumber pods.

Of course, there was still plenty to do for any slugs who wanted more than just relaxation. They could ride on the rollercoaster or take a trampoline exercise class on the jam balloon stretching station. And if they were hungry – Mucus looked over towards the rotten cabbage juice bar and took another sip of his drink – the Hand-Bots really did make a very delicious rotten cabbage cocktail.

It had almost been *too* simple.

He peered out of the window towards the potting shed, where he could see that boy, Scooter McLay, talking with his friends. Cat's words were still ringing in Mucus's ears.

"Just a slug, indeed." Mucus huffed. "How could they say that after everything I've achieved? I could outsmart that dim-witted child again if I *wanted* to." His eyes fell on the wall in front of him. It was filled with press cuttings and awards that Scooter had received. "I could easily come up with better jam inventions than him." His eyes narrowed as he took another sip of his drink. "I wonder what flavour I'd make first?"

Almost as soon as the question was out of his mouth, Mucus felt a tingling sensation as his little body glowed for a moment and his head fizzed with ideas of delicious new jam flavours.

Plant pot jam? No.

Wellington boot jam? No.

Wait a minute! He looked down at his juice and grinned as an idea popped into his head.

"I'll show them what *just a slug* can do!" he snarled as he picked up the remote control and pressed a button with a flourish. "I'm going to make the greatest flavour of jam that the world has ever known!" He beamed as Hand-Bot One approached. "I would like you to find me –" he paused for dramatic effect – "one million rotten cabbages!"

CHAPTER SIX

"And that's how I propose we break into the factory and take it back from the slugs." Daffy stood to the side of the whiteboard propped against the wall of the potting shed, where she'd drawn an elaborate diagram of Boris doing the splits over a laser inside the vents.

"**Squeak**." Boris kissed his biceps, then began stretching.

"Boris is –" Cat watched dubiously as Boris tried to touch his toes and grunted at the effort – "errr ... *good* at yoga, is he?"

"Weeeellll –" Daffy shuffled as the whole team watched Boris – "he could be. With a bit of high-intensity training." She gave Boris a winning smile as Boris attempted the splits, then accidentally released a little poo pellet.

"Umm." Scooter blinked. "Except, we added the lasers to the vents to stop animals like Boris from getting in through them."

"Well, other animals don't have a *chi* like Boris." Daffy raised her eyebrows. "That means *life energy* in yoga-speak. Not to mention his incredible poise, balance and flexibility," she continued defiantly as she drew a series of pictures of Boris on the whiteboard doing a headstand into a backward lunge over a laser and then standing upright on one leg, his front paws pressed together in a perfect tree pose. "See?" She tapped the picture, pretending not to notice as Boris scratched his ear, then wiped the earwax off onto his fur. "Chi."

"Right. OK." Scooter nodded uncertainly. "Well, let's add it to the list of ideas." He glanced over at Fizzbee and she began writing on the blank page of the jam inventions book.

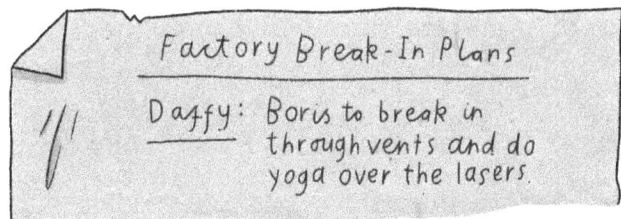

"Scooter?" Fizzbee put the pen down. "Fizzbee has an idea too." She pulled one antenna over her shoulder and wrapped it nervously around her finger.

Scooter's ears pricked up. Fizzbee always had great ideas. If Fizzbee had a solution, then it was going to be something *really* good.

"Yes, Fizz?" he asked eagerly.

"Well ..." she began, her eyes shooting up to meet Scooter's, then back down towards the floor. "Fizzbee is small, like a slug." She put her two fingers together to demonstrate.

"Small. Right. Yes?" Scooter grinned in anticipation.

"So –" Fizzbee spread her arms wide – "maybe Fizzbee could just walk in through the front door and the slugs won't even notice!" She beamed.

"Oh." Scooter tried not to let his smile drop. "Um." He swallowed hard. Fizzbee's idea wasn't quite as creative as he'd been hoping.

"Is that it?" Daffy huffed as she leant against the wall of the shed. "Nothing a bit more, you know, *alieny*?"

"Nope." Fizzbee picked up the pen and began writing down her idea. "It is Fizzbee's *alieny* ideas that caused this whole problem in the first place." She gave a firm shake of her head. "Fizzbee is not using any alieny ideas right now."

Fizzbee: Just walk in and hope the slugs don't notice!

"Squeak, squeak, squeak, squeak, squeak, squeak, squeak," Boris suggested as his paws flailed around descriptively. He stopped and waited for everyone's reactions.

"Ummm." Scooter tilted his head. "I didn't quite…"

"Thank you, Boris." Fizzbee leant forward over the jam inventions book. "I will add your idea to the list."

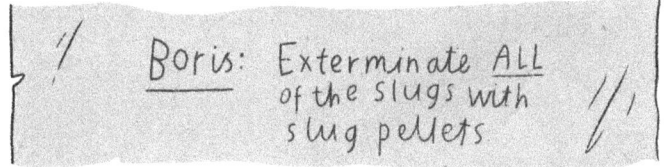

Boris: Exterminate ALL of the slugs with slug pellets

"Oh, Boris!" Daffy clapped her hands. "That's actually not such a bad idea!"

"We are not going to commit mass slug murder!" Scooter leapt to his feet as Fizzbee hastily crossed it off the list.

"Suit yourself," Daffy huffed. "But I don't see anyone else coming up with anything better." She gave Scooter a pointed glare.

"SCOOOOOTTTEEEERRRRRR!"

Scooter turned towards the door of the potting shed in surprise. That sounded like Mum. But she was stuck inside the flat, wasn't she? He poked his head out of the lopsided door and peered up towards the window, where Mum and Dad were waving to him.

"We're – Stuck – Inside – Here!" Dad made an elaborate mime of trying to open a door. "We've been trying to get out but we've only got four bags of jam-apple crisps and a size three slipper to help us." He opened one of the packets of crisps and started eating them. "Actually, we've only got three bags of jam-apple crisps."

"But, Scoot, listen!" Mum continued as she finally managed to lever the window open with the slipper. "We've been thinking that an adult needs to have a reasonable conversation with the slugs. We think that Daffy should go and have a word with them and ask nicely if they'll give our factory back. OK?" They gave Scooter an enthusiastic thumbs up.

"Errr..." Scooter tried to look eager about what was, quite frankly, a completely terrible idea. "O-K. Thanks, Mum and Dad." He smiled just a little too wide, then quickly ducked back inside the potting shed, as Fizzbee added the idea to the list.

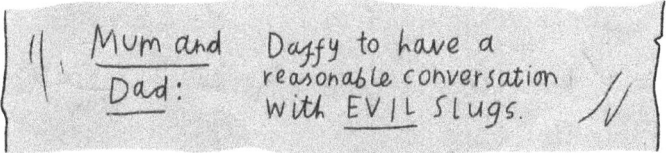

11. Mum and Dad: Daffy to have a reasonable conversation with EVIL slugs.

"Well, that's the worst idea of all!" Cat exploded. "Daffy's never had a reasonable conversation in her life."

"I have!" Daffy snapped. "Haven't I, Boris?"

"**Squeak**." Boris shrugged awkwardly.

Scooter sighed as he looked down the list. The brainstorm definitely wasn't going as well as he'd hoped.

"What about you, Cat?" He raised his eyes hopefully. "Have you got any ideas? Is there anything in that slug encyclopedia about how to sneak past slugs?"

"Nothing *yet*." Cat sighed as she closed the book. "But I guess I could just break in through my *usual* routes." She gave the list of ideas a dismissive wave.

"Your *usual* routes?" Scooter chuckled as he thought of all the times that Cat had turned up unexpectedly. He'd always just assumed that someone had let her in without his noticing.

"Uh-huh." Cat gave him a cheeky wink. "I have my ways."

"What ways?" Daffy frowned. "How exactly do you get in? Because I think as Head of Security, I ought to know."

"Well, let's just say that there are quite a few old jam pipes that aren't used any more." Cat tapped her nose secretly. "And if you know how to get into them – like I do – then there are a couple of ways to get inside."

Scooter's face lit up. If Cat had been regularly breaking

into the factory all this time through the disused jam pipes, then maybe getting the remote control from the dastardly slug wouldn't be so hard! After all, when it came to a stealth mission, Cat's incredible climbing and somersaulting abilities meant she had all the right skills.

"Well, that's brilliant!" Scooter beamed. "Let's definitely add that one to the list!"

He watched as Fizzbee wrote it down.

Cat: Break in via her usual routes.

"I think we should start with Cat's idea." Scooter smiled as Fizzbee passed him the jam inventions book. He leant back on the potting table to stabilize himself, then carefully lifted

Factory Break-In Plans

Daffy: Boris to break in through vents and do yoga over the lasers.

~~Boris: Exterminate ALL of the slugs with slug pellets.~~

Fizzbee: Just walk in and hope the slugs don't notice!

Mum and Dad: Daffy to have a reasonable conversation with EVIL slugs.

Cat: Break in via usual routes.

the book for everyone to see. "And if that doesn't work, then I guess we'll just have to, err, go back to the other options." He studied the list and pretended not to notice as Daffy heaved Boris out of the splits. "So, let's just really hope that this works," he murmured under his breath.

"Brilliant!" Cat began limbering up. "Don't you worry, Scoot." She stretched one arm over her head, then the other. "I'll be back here with that remote control in a jiffy. By the time Daffy says, 'Where did Cat go?' I'll already be inside the factory."

"What do you mean, by the time Daffy says – oh—" Scooter stopped talking as he turned back to the now-empty spot where Cat had been standing just moments ago.

"Well, wait a minute." Daffy stared at the factory. "Where *did* she go?"

CHAPTER SEVEN

"I'm sorry, Scooter." Cat's head poked back through the door of the potting shed a short while later. She was covered from head to toe in slug slime. "They've blocked all of the old jam pipes with slime! I tried to push my way through, but I kept getting stuck. I had no idea that slug slime was so sticky!" She paused as her gaze fell on the slug encyclopedia again. "Maybe I need to be more specific. There must be something in here about getting through slug slime." She sat down and started reading.

"Good thinking." Scooter watched as Fizzbee put a cross through Cat's idea on the list.

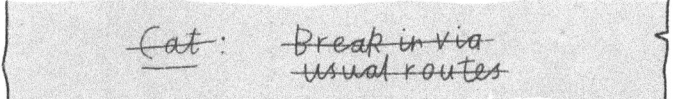

"Scooter, we don't have the first hope of getting inside the factory without your ideas." Daffy stroked Boris sadly as she looked at the list of ideas over his shoulder. "Cat's plan was the best one. Maybe we should just give up until your creativity comes back."

Scooter leant on the windowsill of the potting shed and stared out towards the jam factory as he tried to ignore the knot in his tummy when he thought about whether his creativity would *ever* come back.

All of his creativity and ideas had gone into creating that magical building that stood before him. He'd worked so hard on it.

In fact, it wasn't just Scooter who had worked hard, it was every single person in this room.

Fizzbee had worked tirelessly on every invention with him.

Cat had grown and tended so many of the plants with such attention and care.

Even Daffy and Boris patrolled the factory every day as if they were knights protecting a beloved castle.

Scooter stood up, his fists clenched.

Well, he wasn't going to let a bunch of slimy slugs take it from them, whether he had his creativity or not!

"You're right, these ideas aren't perfect." He turned towards the team as he held up the list. "But they're ours! And we need to see them through! Maybe they won't work. Or maybe they

will. Maybe they'll open up a whole new way to get inside. But whatever, we can't give up now! We've got to try." He met Cat, Daffy and Boris's eyes as each one of them stood to join him, then turned to Fizzbee, who was hovering towards him in her jam tart. "Are you with me?" he asked.

"Always, Scooter." She took her position beside his shoulder.

Nobody noticed that Scooter's hair was standing just a little straighter from his head.

"This is our factory!" Fizzbee punched her fist into the palm of her hand. "And we will defend it!" Scooter turned to Boris, his face burning with the glow of fresh determination. "It's time for you to suit up." He pointed down to a little hazmat suit as Boris took a deep breath and got into a downward guinea pig yoga position. "We need you to warrior-pose your way past those lasers."

"Is that it?" Mucus sneered as the Hand-Bots dropped one fresh cabbage leaf on the floor in front of him. "I said one million rotten cabbages! Not one leaf!" The Hand-Bots spread out their hands apologetically before Hand-Bot One jerked its thumb towards the café, where at least twenty slugs queued impatiently at the rotten cabbage juice bar. It seemed that rotten cabbages were in high demand.

Mucus let out a heavy sigh.

There really were a *lot* of slugs here. A lot of slugs with *big* appetites. And if there were no rotten cabbages for them to eat, then Mucus was quite sure that they'd eat whatever else they could find.

"Urgh! You're not supposed to eat that, get off!" Mucus shooed away a small slug who had started chowing down on the leg of his sun-lounger.

Ploop. The little slug shrugged, then began munching on a guinea pig dropping on the floor.

Mucus looked at the slimy leg of his sun-lounger, then turned to look at the wriggling, writhing bodies all over the place and couldn't help thinking, just for a moment, that his slug café and wellness spa had looked better before there had been *quite* so many slugs inside it.

"I really do need those rotten cabbages," he sighed.

Rotten cabbages would solve all of his problems. He could show those humans, especially Scooter, his superior jam-making skills *and* it would provide plenty of food for the slugs. Then they'd stop eating everything in sight and his wondrous slug café and wellness spa wouldn't be quite as munched on and slimed over.

"But how can I get hold of a million rotten cabbages?" he muttered as he drank his rotten cabbage juice and, for a moment, a tiny memory popped into his head. A memory of slithering past a load of rotten fruit and vegetables. But before he had a chance to grasp hold of that thought, he felt the tingling sensation again and with a whizz and a fizz, at least twenty other ideas hurtled into his mind.

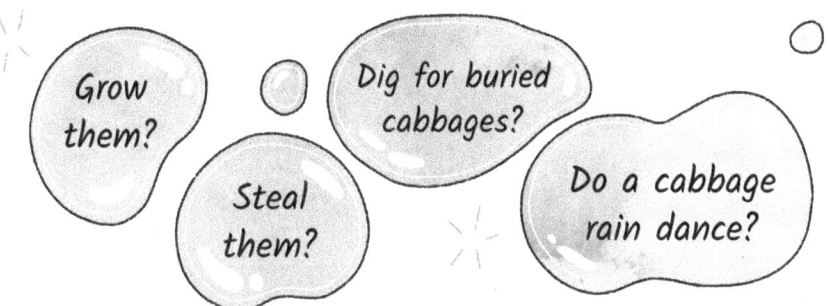

Grow them?

Dig for buried cabbages?

Steal them?

Do a cabbage rain dance?

His eyes darted from left to right as he tried to make sense of all the thoughts and ideas, his little slug body glowing with the effort.

Ask a human?

"Aha!" he giggled evilly. "I bet those humans know how to get hold of rotten cabbages." He rubbed his two tentacles together in anticipation. "Maybe I just need to interrogate one of them."

Scooter watched Fizzbee cross another item off the list of ideas as Boris hovered through the sky towards them, a rope of slime attaching his leg to a jam balloon.

"Squeak!" he uttered feebly.

"I'm coming, Boris!" Daffy ran to catch the balloon.

"It is up to Fizzbee now, Scooter." Fizzbee put the pen down, before hovering in her jam tart up to the windowsill. "I have a sign to help." She pointed to a helpful sign around her neck.

> I am a slug. NOT an alien.

"Are you sure about the sign, Fizz?" Scooter leant down to talk to her at the windowsill, smiling as she gave him a slug-like wriggle in reply. "Hmm, OK. Just remember to try and act like a bog-standard slug!"

"Yes, Scooter." Fizzbee took a deep breath, then let her legs dangle over the windowsill as she looked down at the line of slugs below.

"Good luck, Fizzbee!" Cat glanced up from the slug encyclopedia.

Fizzbee gave Scooter one last smile, then dropped out of the window.

"Wheeeeeeeeeee!" she squealed as she landed on the floor beside a surprised-looking slug. "Hello," she introduced herself, before jiggling theatrically. "I am a slug. Look, I have a sign!" She pointed to the little sign around her neck. "I am definitely not an alien. My name is Fizzbee. What's your name?"

Squelch, the slug replied before peering suspiciously up towards the window.

"Scooter?" Cat's head darted up from the slug encyclopedia as Scooter ducked back. "The more I read of this book, the more I can't help feeling that Fizzbee's plan really *isn't* going to work."

"Oh, really?" Scooter had to admit that he'd thought the exact same thing.

"You needed a book to figure that out?" Daffy called over her shoulder as she tried to untangle Boris's leg from a sticky trail of slug slime.

"Well –" Cat ignored her as she held up the encyclopedia for Scooter to see – "it says here slugs communicate through their slime trails." She gave the book a little tap. "And I don't think Fizzbee knows Slimeish, does she?" Scooter shook his head as he peeked back out of the window. Fizzbee was still trying to chat to the slugs as she jauntily followed the line into the factory.

"Maybe we'll get lucky?" He gave a doubtful shrug.

"Yeah, maybe." Cat crossed her fingers.

They didn't have to wait long to find out. Less than five minutes later and …

They bolted back up, just in time to see Fizzbee getting blasted out of the factory from one of the jam squirters.

"EEEEEEEEEEEEEEEEEEEE EEEEEEEEEE!"

Donk.

She landed in a plant pot just behind them.

"Fizz, are you OK?" Scooter rushed towards her, but he didn't need to worry; Fizzbee was already climbing out of it.

"I'm sorry, Scooter. Fizzbee did not get very far." She gave her head a little rub at the edge of the pot. "But Fizzbee has made lots of new slug friends – and, Scooter…?" She hesitated. "They did not seem *so* bad." She hopped down from the pot, walked towards the list of break-in ideas and crossed off her entry.

> Fizzbee: ~~Just walk in and hope the slugs don't notice!~~

"Fizzbee is wondering if talking to the leader is not such a bad idea." She pointed to the last item on the list of break-in ideas as everyone peered down over her shoulder.

Daffy to have a reasonable conversation with the evil slugs.

"I agree." Cat tucked the slug encyclopedia under her arm. "At least you don't need to speak Slimeish with him."

"But I don't want to go into the slug-infested factory!" Daffy wailed.

CHAPTER EIGHT

Scooter, Fizzbee, Cat and Boris watched from the window of the potting shed as Daffy approached the front door of the factory. She stopped, shot them a nervous glance, then took a deep breath and gave the front door the lightest of knocks.

Tap tap.

There was no reply.

"Oh, well." Daffy turned back to the potting shed with a shrug. "It looks like there's no answer. I guess we'll just have to come up with…"

SCCCHHLLLL OOPPPPPPPPPPP.

The front door squelched loudly as it was pushed open. Gloopy, gooey slime dripped and oozed from the doorway.

"Did you know that slug slime is actually a liquid crystal?" Cat whispered as they all craned their necks to see inside. "It works as a lubricant so that slugs can get over spiky things without getting hurt, but it also works as a glue to help slugs climb walls." As she spoke, Hand-Bot One rose up from behind the door. In the palm of its hand was the haughty slug in the bow tie, who was drinking some kind of disgusting-looking brown drink through a curly straw.

The slug raised his half-lidded eyes slowly towards Daffy.

"Can I help you?" he asked, pompously.

"Oh. Errrrr. Hello." Daffy tugged nervously at her sleeves. "I'm here to have a *reasonable conversation* with you."

"OK." The slug stifled a yawn before his eyes darted just for a moment towards the potting shed and Scooter caught a flicker of something crafty and cunning.

"Right. Well –" Daffy crossed, then uncrossed her arms – "we would very much appreciate it if you wouldn't mind just shoving right—"

"Perhaps ..." the slug interrupted her, "you'd like to come in to discuss this further?" He gave Daffy an oily smile as Hand-Bot One moved to welcome her inside.

"Oh." Daffy shot another anxious glance back towards the potting shed.

"I can offer you a rotten cabbage juice?"

The slug nodded towards his glass, then frowned. "Actually, we're a bit low on it right now. I saw some bottles of something called Jam Fizz lying around. It won't be as nice, of course, but perhaps you could have some of that?"

"Well, I must say that's very kind of you." Daffy's face brightened as she took a cautious step forward. "Boris and I aren't normally allowed to eat any of the jam when we're *on duty*." She gave her hair a little pat, then leant forward and whispered, "You know, Boris even has to wear a hazmat suit?"

"Well, that sounds positively ghastly." The slug drew in a long breath. "You'd better come inside and tell me all about it. I'm Mucus, by the way," he introduced himself.

"Mucus Vane."

"Pleased to meet you, Mucus." Daffy stepped inside the factory and Scooter had one last glimpse of her, before Mucus looked back and gave him a devilish wink and the factory door squelched shut.

Scooter, Fizzbee, Cat and Boris all turned towards each other uneasily.

"That seemed way too easy." Scooter stared hard at the closed door, his stomach fluttering. "I think that slug – Mucus – he's up to something."

"Yeah." Cat bit her lip. "He seemed a bit…"

"Slimy." Fizzbee finished her sentence for her.

"**Squeak**." Boris released a poo pellet.

"Do you think he seriously wants to have a *reasonable conversation*?" Cat voiced what they were all wondering, their eyes never leaving the front door. "And how long do they take?"

"Well, if my mum's anything to go by,

they can take *ages*." Scooter gave a knowing shake of his head. "But I've got a funny feeling that…"

He stopped talking as a postcard was slid out from underneath the front door.

Fizzbee hovered over, picked it up and returned with it in her hand.

> To those foolish children in the potting shed,
> Deliver one million rotten cabbages to me and she will be released.

Attached to it was a Polaroid photo of Daffy surrounded by some big thuggish slugs.

"Squeeeeeaaaaaakkkk!" Boris wailed.

"The slugs have kidnapped Daffy!" Scooter cried. "But for a million rotten cabbages? Seriously? They've got a whole factory of plants! That doesn't make any sense!"

"It does, Scooter, when you read up about slugs." Cat lifted the slug encyclopedia out from under her arm and opened it up for them to see.

"Slugs enjoy eating decomposing fruit and vegetables more than when they're fresh." She pointed to a diagram. "Did you know that if there were no slugs then there would be a lot more rubbish?" she continued. "Slugs love eating rubbish!"

"Really?" Scooter peered down at the book. "But if they prefer rotten fruit and vegetables, why are they trying to take over the jam factory?"

"It's not easy to be a slug." Cat turned to another page of the book.

Slug Predators.

"Lots of animals and birds want to eat them. And humans hate slugs so much they try to kill them with slug pellets or eggshells or salt. I guess the factory is a safe place, even if it doesn't have their favourite food."

"Oh." Scooter turned back towards the window and stared down at the line of slugs. He'd never really thought about what it was like to be a slug before. It probably wasn't all that great when so many animals and birds wanted to eat you. He peered up at the sky overhead. Scooter had been chased by a seagull once himself when he'd eaten some of Fizzbee's

Shrinking Strawberry Jam. It wasn't an experience he wanted to repeat anytime soon.

He paused.

Maybe he'd been going about this the wrong way. Perhaps instead of thinking about how to get the slugs out of the factory, he needed to think about what it was that the slugs *wanted*.

"The funny thing is –" he used his right hand to slowly turn the page back to the diagram of a slug's favourite food – "we actually *do* have their favourite food in the factory." He sat up, his hair bolting out from his head like a resplendent, bristling bog brush. "This might actually have given me…"

"Scooter?" Fizzbee stared around his head, her eyes opening wide. "Scooter is having ideas!" she squealed.

Meanwhile, back in the factory, Mucus was interrogating Daffy.

"I'll never talk. Not in a million years. I'm not telling you *anything*!" Daffy squirmed as Hand-Bot One lowered Mucus towards her and he slithered onto her shoulder. "Wait! Hold on, hold on." She pulled her face as far away from her shoulder as she could manage. "Maybe I was a bit hasty. Please don't slime me!"

"Don't *slime* you?" Mucus frowned. "Why not? Slime's lovely." He looked out at the slug café and wellness spa. It was getting slimier by the second. He watched as some dripped down from a strawberry plant. "In small doses, anyway," he added.

"No, it's not!" Daffy scrunched her face up in disgust. "It's sticky and gloopy and yucky!"

"How dare you!" Mucus pulled himself up to his full slug height. "I'll show you *sticky*!" He slithered onto her neck.

"EWWWWWWWWW!" Daffy screeched. "No, Mucus, please no! I take it all back. I'm sure slug slime's lovely really."

"And *gloopy*!" Mucus wriggled up to her ear.

"Aaaaaaaaaaarrrrrrrgggggggghhhhhhhhhh!" Daffy wailed.

"And *yucky*!" He squirmed onto her cheek.

"Oooh!" Daffy giggled. "Actually, that tickles!" Mucus wriggled a little. "Ha!" Daffy snorted.

Mucus wriggled again.

"Hee hee heeeeee!" Daffy erupted into

squeals of uncontrollable laughter. "Oh no!" She bent over double, chortling and chuckling, her arms thrown around her belly. "Oh, please stop! I can't take it any more!" she gurgled. "I'll tell you anything you want to know, Mucus! Please just no more. It's too tickly!"

"I don't need to know anything." Mucus slid back down to her shoulder with a dismissive shake of his head. "I'm just holding you hostage until your friends deliver one million rotten cabbages."

"Oh." Daffy's shoulders dropped as her gaze fell on the sun-loungers. "Well, then, Mucus, me old pal." She sidled in towards him. "Didn't you say something about Jam Fizz?"

CHAPTER NINE

Scooter, Fizzbee, Cat and Boris scrambled out of the patrol buggy as they reached a large barn at the back of the factory filled with a giant mound of rotting fruit and vegetables.

"Whoa, Scooter!" Cat stared up at a giant chute that dropped into the barn. "I didn't realize that the compost pile had got so big!"

"I know." Scooter scrunched up his nose. "It's one of the problems with growing all of the fruit and vegetables inside the factory. The compost heap just seems to keep getting bigger and bigger. Actually, finding a better way of disposing of the plant waste was on my to-do list."

"You know, the slugs could help you with that." Cat gave her book a little tap as Boris rolled his eyes at yet another slug fact. "Did you know that slug poo is an amazing plant fertilizer? The slugs could eat all of these rotten fruit and vegetables and turn it into fertilizer. Plus, slugs eat at least double their weight every day. It probably wouldn't take all that long to get through all of this."

"I was wondering the same thing." Scooter picked up a yellowing Brussels sprout. "But I think we've got to get into the factory first. And for that we need a million rotten cabbages for Mucus. Luckily, we've easily got that here…" His eyes twinkled merrily. "Because Brussels sprouts are basically tiny cabbages!"

"So, your plan is to give Mucus … *exactly what he wants*?" Cat looked unconvinced. "But don't we need to get the slugs out of the factory? Rather than giving them a reason to stay?"

"Sort of." Scooter tossed the Brussels sprout into the trailer at the back of Daffy's patrol buggy. "But we need to get *inside* the factory

before we can get the slugs *out*." He lifted one finger on his right hand. "That's going to be Challenge One." He lifted a second finger. "Challenge Two will be freeing the Hand-Bots by taking that remote control from Mucus." He lifted his third finger. "And Challenge Three…?" He raised his eyebrows and smiled. "That will be getting all of the slugs out of the factory and cleaning up in time for the hygiene inspection."

"Oh." Cat's brow cleared. "You know, it doesn't seem so bad when you break it down like that, Scoot."

"I think you were right. My creativity has been blocked because I've been trying to solve too many problems at once." Scooter smiled. "If I focus on one thing at a time, then maybe it will come back?"

"This is verrrrry good, Scooter!" Fizzbee patted his ear approvingly from his shoulder. "And we can help you with each challenge too."

"I'm counting on it," Scooter grinned.

"You know, Scoot." Cat lifted her book. "When it comes to getting the slugs out of the factory, there's loads of information in here about all the things they don't like. Did you know that slugs hate strong-smelling plants, like lavender? So, I was wondering, why don't we stink them out with some Relaxing Lavender Jam?"

"That's a great idea!" Scooter exclaimed. "Your knowledge of slugs and plants is going to really help us once we're inside. Maybe we should pack some jars just in case."

"Squeak, squeak, squeak, squeak, squeak, squeak, squeak?" Boris crossed his paws.

"I...?" Scooter looked to Fizzbee for an explanation.

"Boris is wondering which challenge is to save Daffy?" Fizzbee translated.

"Oh, of course." Scooter nodded in

understanding as Cat picked up Boris and held him in the crook of her arm. "Saving Daffy is part of Challenge Two." Scooter gave him a reassuring stroke. "She'll be safe as soon as we've stopped Mucus."

"Squeak." Boris snuggled into Cat's arm.

"OK, great. Well, let's focus on Challenge One for now." Scooter looked at the trailer on the back of Daffy's patrol buggy and grinned. "It's sprout time."

Back inside the factory, Mucus sat beside Daffy on a sun-lounger, towels wrapped around their heads, slices of cucumber over their eyes, as they sipped their drinks.

"Well, I must say this is very nice, Mucus." Daffy lifted the cucumber slices from her eyes, then took the tiny umbrella from her drink and tucked into the cherry attached to it. "And err..." She peered out at the factory. "I like what you've done with the place. It's errr, well ... it's very..." She bit her lip as Mucus lifted the cucumber slices from his tentacles and followed her gaze. The jam brooks and streams, half as full as they had been, were filled with wriggling, writhing slugs. The giant massaging paintbrushes were covered in oozing, dripping slime. And as for the rotten cabbage juice bar? At least twenty slugs were eating the sign!

"If you'd just seen it an hour ago..." Mucus sighed. "It was much nicer then. But, well, slugs do like a to eat a lot."

"Mmm," Daffy murmured, before taking an awkward glug of her Jam Fizz.

"Oh, let's face it ... it's *ruined*!" Mucus let out a cry of frustration as the lovely picture he'd painted of humans begging him to be allowed inside his wonderful spa dissolved before his eyes. "I just wanted to show everyone that slugs are not just some common garden pest!" He began to cry hot slimy tears. "But now I'm looking around and even *I* think they're pests!" He took a sip of his juice and hiccupped. "What's the point?"

"Oh, Mucus." Daffy went to put her arm around him, then stopped and very hesitantly gave him a little pat with her finger. "Ooooh, your skin is so smooth." She rubbed her finger along his back.

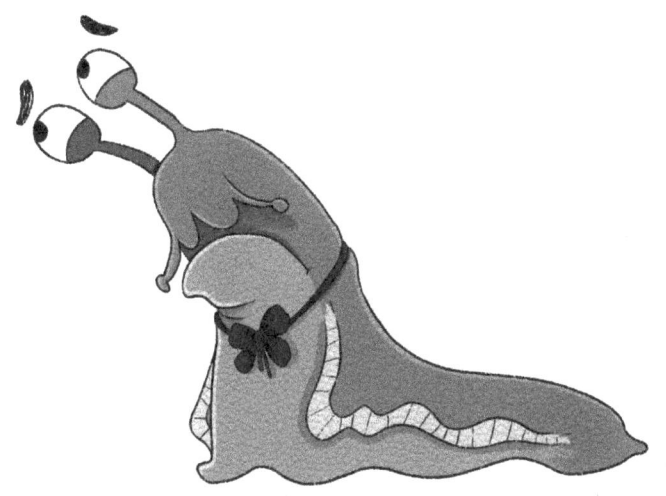

"Thank you." Mucus sniffled, then wiped a tear with his sensory tentacle. "I try. You might not have noticed when I slimed you earlier, what with all of the, ahem, screaming and giggling, but if you put a bit of my slime on your face, it will really help your complexion."

"Really?" Daffy wiped a little of his slime onto her face. "Oh, yes – it's lovely!" She began rubbing it all over her face like a mask. "You're not like other slugs, are you, Mucus?" She gave him a friendly little pat, then spread yet more slime onto her face. "I mean, apart from the talking. You seem a bit smarter if I'm honest."

"I am!" Mucus turned to her in surprise. Nobody had ever noticed how smart he was before.

"I don't think there are many slugs that could take control of the jam factory." She gave him a little nudge. "I tried to break in for years and didn't manage it. And to turn the place into a slug café and wellness spa, well that really is quite a special achievement." She smiled down into his eyes.

"Oh, Daffy!" Mucus looked up at her adoringly. "Do you really mean it?" He paused as he took a long look at the wall of Scooter's press cuttings and awards. "You know, I've even had an idea for the greatest-ever jam," he sniffled. "Much better than anything that Scooter boy could come up with. Do you want to hear it?"

"You know I do." Daffy grinned as she sidled in.

"It's …" Mucus paused dramatically, "Rotten Cabbage Jam!" He clapped his tentacles together excitedly. "Isn't it wonderful?"

"Rotten Cabbage?" Daffy raised her eyebrows hesitantly. "Riiiight. Because you *like* … *rotten* things, do you?"

"Oh, yes." Mucus nodded enthusiastically. "Rotten cabbage is a slug's favourite food! I'm going to set the jam world alight with my new jam flavour."

Daffy shrugged. "Well, you've definitely come up with something very original there, Mucus. I've heard of worse ideas." She gave him a friendly pat, pulled the cucumber slices back over her eyes and relaxed into her sun-lounger.

"Thank you, Daffy." Mucus peered at her sideways. Daffy was the first person who'd ever really listened to him. The first person who'd ever tried to understand him. She liked his slug slime. She'd even called him *smart!*

"Daffy Dodgy…" Mucus pulled himself up as Daffy lifted the cucumber slices again with a quizzical glance. "Will you do me the honour of becoming –" he straightened his tie with his sensory tentacle – "my best friend?" He gazed hopefully into her eyes.

"Oh, Mucus!" Daffy put her hand to her heart before her smile dropped just a little.

"Except, um, I've already got a best friend." She pulled a photo of Boris out of her pocket and showed it to Mucus, quickly shoving it back when she saw Mucus's crushed face.

"But I can still be *your* best friend if you'd like? And maybe you can be my *second*-best friend?"

"Oh, Daffy! A thousand times yes!" Mucus beamed as he and Daffy clinked glasses together in celebration.

"You know, Mucus, me old pal –" Daffy took another slurp of her Jam Fizz – "if your favourite food is really rotten fruit and vegetables, then I'm not sure that this factory is the right place for you. I mean, all of the fruit here is fresh." She peered around the place. "Do you think there might be a better place for your slug café and wellness spa?"

Mucus nodded. "I've been wondering the same thing. But where can we find a constant supply of rotten fruit and vegetables?"

Daffy sighed as she gazed around the factory. She looked at the banana trees, the strawberry walls, the brooks and streams, until finally, her eyes rested on the compost chute.

"I haven't got a clue, Mucus." She shook her head and pulled the cucumber slices back over her eyes.

Scooter, Fizzbee, Cat and Boris crouched inside the trailer, hidden beneath an enormous pile of rotten Brussels sprouts.

"Is this really the best way to get inside, Scoot?" Cat held her nose. "It smells like old feet in here."

"**Squeak**," Boris agreed, wrinkling his nose in disgust at the sprouts.

"It's the only idea that I'm sure will work." Scooter ducked right down, though he couldn't help agreeing that it was really stinky hiding inside a pile of sprouts. "There's no way that the slugs will turn away a whole trailer of their favourite food!" He met Fizzbee's eyes. "OK, Fizz, we're ready."

Fizzbee nodded nervously, then cautiously hovered out from their hiding place. Her eyes darted from left to right as she flew up towards the front door of the jam factory. She gave it a tentative knock, then dived back to the safety of the sprouts, where they all waited for the door to open.

"What is Scooter's plan when we get inside?" she whispered as she squeezed under a leaf.

"Well, then we move on to Challenge Two," Scooter whispered back, "Getting the remote control and freeing the Hand-Bots so that we can stop Mucus."

"Yes?" Fizzbee waited for him to explain as Scooter passed some Brussels sprout leaves to her and Boris. "And how is Scooter planning to do that?"

"Well, Cat and I are too big to disguise ourselves," he continued. "So, we'll have to stay hidden in here. But if you and Boris dress up in these sprout leaves, then I'm sure that you could get across the factory to the remote control."

SQUEEEEELLLLLLLLCCCCCHHHHHHHH.

They all dived down deeper as they heard the front door slowly open.

Squelch squiiiiiiiisssshhhhhh.

There was the sound of a happy bubble of slime overhead and the next thing Scooter felt was the rumbling of the trailer as it was slowly pulled inside the factory.

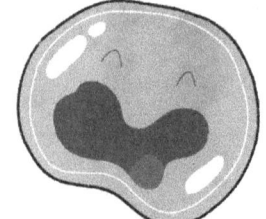

CHAPTER TEN

Scooter peered out at the factory through a tiny hole in the bottom of the trailer.

There were slugs *everywhere*.

Slugs having a bubble bath in the jam.

Slugs having a massage from a giant (and very slimy) paintbrush.

Slugs riding on the rollercoaster.

Even slugs bouncing on the jam balloon stretching station as if it were a trampoline!

There were thousands of them.

They wriggled and jiggled, squirmed and squiggled over the *entire* factory.

Strawberries were splatted on the floor amongst trails of slime. The leaves of the banana trees were brown and curling. The hedgerows of blueberry bushes, raspberry canes and watermelons had barely any leaves on them.

And as for the Brussels sprout batteries? There were so few Brussels sprouts left that it couldn't be long before the factory was plunged into total darkness.

The slugs were eating everything in sight! There was no doubt about it. This was an absolute *disaster.*

"Argh…" Scooter's hand flew to his mouth as a jam jar trundled past him on a conveyor belt, at least five slugs fidgeting and frolicking inside it. "Everything's completely ruined!" He let out a strangled gasp. "Even if we can stop Mucus and get the slugs out, how are we ever going to fix all this? And what about the hygiene inspection?!"

"One challenge at a time, Scooter." Fizzbee held one finger up as Scooter tried to compose himself. "This is Challenge Two." She met his eyes as Cat nodded along reassuringly. "Get the remote control and free the Hand-Bots."

"Right." Scooter blew out his cheeks. "OK. Challenge Two." He looked back at the factory, trying to ignore the slimy chaos and focus on finding Mucus and the remote control. Finally, his gaze fell on the Hand-Bots. They were just above the Banana Jam bubble bath and they seemed to be making a cocktail.

"That's where he'll be." Scooter nodded towards them. "Remember Mucus was drinking that weird drink earlier? I bet he's got the Hand-Bots making him another one." He turned towards Fizzbee and Boris. Fizzbee had a sprout leaf on her head, her two antennae sticking out from beneath it. Boris had tucked a cabbage leaf into his collar like a cape. "It's up to you now," he instructed them. "Just get to Mucus, nab the remote control and then bring it back here to me. OK?"

"Yes, Scooter." Fizzbee nodded, her little face full of determination.

"**Squeak**." Boris gave a Brussels sprout a little punch to show them that he meant business.

Scooter watched as Fizzbee and Boris crept out of the trailer, before ducking and diving their way across the factory.

"Hopefully we won't have to wait in here too much longer," he whispered to Cat as he watched their progress through the little peephole. "We just need to stay hidden until they get back."

"Errrrr, Scooter?" Cat patted his arm nervously then pointed behind the trailer. "I think there might just be one problem with your plan." Scooter gasped as he saw a tidal wave of slithering slugs sliming towards them. "We're hiding underneath the slug's favourite food." Cat slowly pulled out a jar of Relaxing Lavender Jam out of her pocket as they both stared wide-eyed at the oncoming wave. "And they're looking mighty hungry!"

"You know, Daffy –" Mucus squelched happily on his sun-lounger – "I'm so pleased that we got talking. I really was expecting some kind of sneaky break-in attempt. But you've shown me that humans lack a lot less charm than I thought."

"Absolutely, Mucus." Daffy straightened the towel on her head, then sat up as she tried to work out if that was a compliment or not. "About the getting-talking bit, I mean." She shrugged. "I told Scooter that I should just come in here and have a reasonable conversation with you. I said, *'Scooter, I'm telling you, we just need to make friends with that lovely little slug.'*"

"You're so wise, Daffy," Mucus mused as Hand-Bot One passed him another rotten cabbage juice. "You really should be the one who runs the factory, you know. That Scooter sounds like a nincompoop."

"Oh, Mucus, you devil!" Daffy giggled as Hand-Bot Two passed her a fluffy robe and a pair of slippers.

"You know what …" Mucus hesitated as he spied something rather strange over by a vat of jam hair gel. There appeared to be a furry-legged cabbage running towards them. He looked at his rotten cabbage juice. Maybe he'd overdone it a bit. "I think…" He hesitated again as, seemingly from nowhere, a Brussels sprout hovered towards them. "Errr, Daffy?" He spoke out of the corner of his mouth. "Is it just me or is there a flying Brussels sprout and a cabbage with legs over there?" He pointed with his tentacles towards them.

"What's that, Mucus?" Daffy followed his gaze. "Oh." Her eyes flared wide for a moment, before she composed herself and took an innocent slurp of her drink. "I don't see anything."

Scooter and Cat ducked down as far as they could and listened to the *munch, crunch* and *scrunch* of the thousands of hungry little slugs champing on the rotten Brussels sprouts just above them.

"I hope Fizz and Boris hurry up and get that remote control." Cat wiped a drip of slime off her cheek, her eyes darting up. "I'm not sure how long we can stay hidden inside here." She opened the jar of Relaxing Lavender Jam as quietly as she could. "At least we've got this if we need to fend them off."

Scooter followed her gaze up to the thin layer of Brussels sprouts above them. It really wasn't going to last much longer. He turned back to the peephole in the trailer and searched desperately for any signs that Fizzbee and Boris's mission was proving successful.

"I think I can see them." His eyes narrowed as he saw a furry-legged cabbage duck behind a vat of jam hair gel, closely followed by a flying Brussels sprout. "They've nearly reached the Hand-Bots!"

He pressed his eye further against the peephole as *something else* caught his eye.

Something unexpected.

The Hand-Bots had passed down the gross brown cocktail, presumably to Mucus, and now they were filling a champagne glass with Jam Fizz.

Who was that for?

He watched, his heart beating a little harder

as Hand-Bot One lifted the glass, revealing...

"Daffy's having a cocktail with Mucus!" Scooter stared in disbelief as Daffy, wearing a fluffy robe and slippers, a face mask and a towel around her head, took a long luxurious slurp of her drink, then chatted with Mucus. "It looks like they're friends!" he cried. "She's laughing! And giggling! Hold on, didn't he kidnap her?" But before Scooter had a chance to make any sense of the scene in front of him, the furry-legged cabbage bolted towards Daffy. "Oh no!" he gasped. "I think Boris might be about to give the game away." He watched as Boris threw off his disguise and began squeaking furiously at Daffy as, at exactly the same moment, the flying Brussels sprout dived down towards Mucus.

"Scooter –" Cat urgently nudged him in the ribs, then pointed up to where thousands of little slug eyes peered down at them – "we've been rumbled."

"Ah." Scooter gave all of the slugs a friendly wave as a drip of slime fell onto his neck and Cat wafted the open jar of Lavender Jam towards them warily. "Errrr … hello."

"Squeak!"

Mucus turned as some kind of enormous slug, with frankly the most terrible complexion and an embarrassingly furry slime trail, threw a cabbage leaf from its back and started squeaking at Daffy angrily.

"Squeak, squeak, squeak, squeak, squeak, squeak, SQUEAK!"

"Daffy? *Who* is this?" Mucus demanded, just seconds before the flying Brussels sprout dived down towards him and began trying to wrestle the remote control out of his sensory tentacles. "What's going on here?" He jostled with the flying Brussels sprout, knocking a leaf off its head to reveal the little alien that had tried to break in earlier. "Hand-Bots!" he screeched as Hand-Bot One zipped down, cupped Fizzbee in its fist, then padlocked her inside a very convenient tiny cage. Mucus had to admit, the Hand-Bots really were *very* helpful. Perhaps one day he could invent some *slime-bots*? But before he had a moment to ponder his wonderful new invention idea, there was a commotion over by the trailer of rotten Brussels sprouts. "What's happening over there?" His eyes narrowed as Scooter and Cat poked their heads out sheepishly from inside the trailer. "What are *you* doing in here?" he roared, his happy slime bubble well and truly popped as he looked from Scooter and Cat, to Fizzbee, to Boris, his eyes flaring angrily as he finally turned to Daffy. "Was all of this just a trick? You were just distracting me while your *real* friends broke in?"

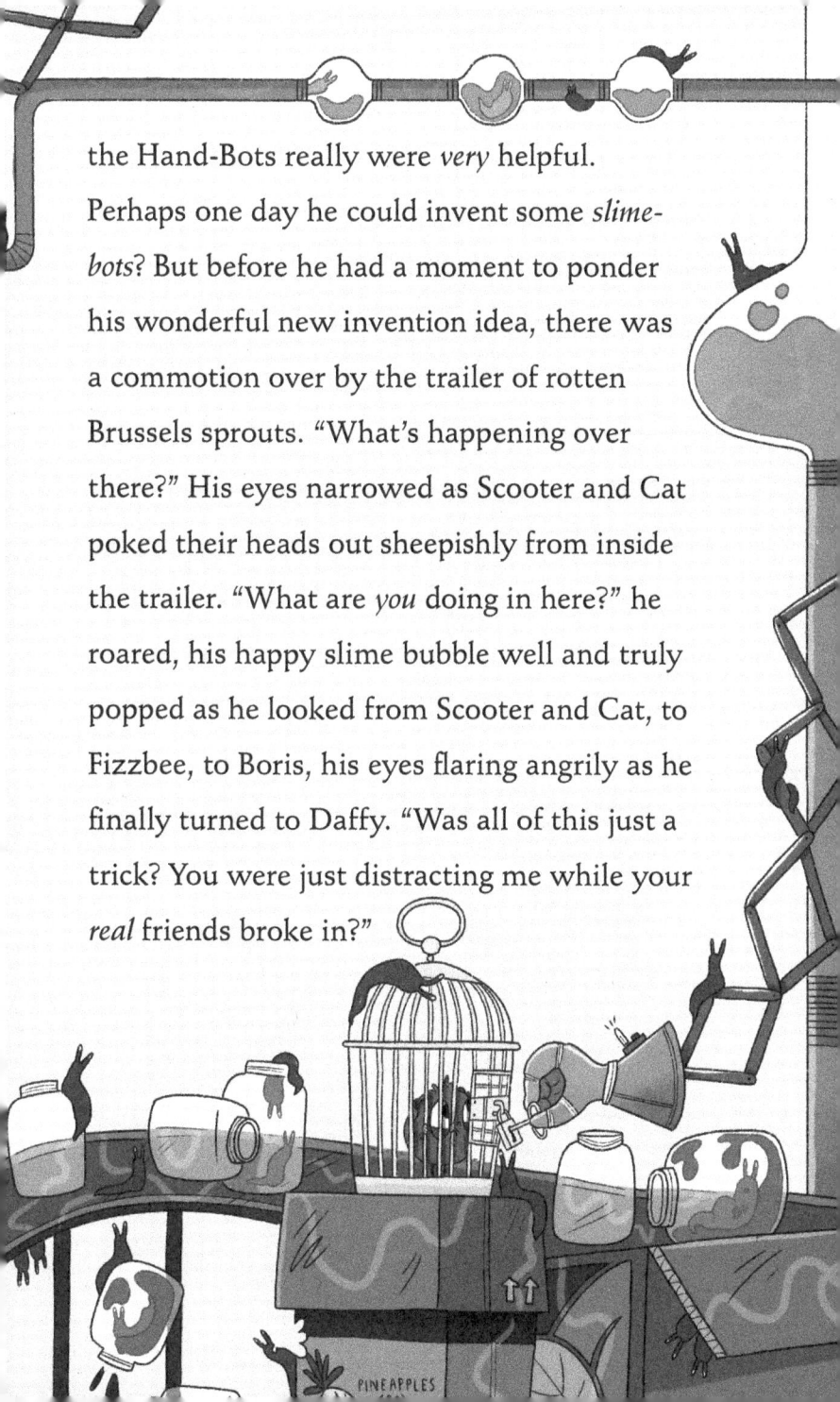

"Now, Mucus, me old chum." Daffy put her hands up as Boris jumped into her lap and stared at Mucus territorially. "This really isn't what it looks like."

"Don't worry, Daffy, we'll save you!" Cat's voice rang out as she jumped out of the trailer and bolted towards Mucus, an open jar of Relaxing Lavender Jam held aloft. "You need to leave this factory right now. Or I'll be forced to use *this*." She wafted it in front of his nose.

"You'll be forced to use *jam*?" Mucus blinked. "What for?"

"This isn't just any jam!" Cat raised her eyebrows. "It's *Lavender Jam*!" She wafted it towards him again.

No one reacted.

"Well, I suppose it's not my favourite." Mucus shrugged.

"But wait! Slugs hate lavender!" Cat put the jar down, then pulled the slug encyclopedia out of her pocket. "It says it right here."

"Well, quite frankly, that's a terrible plan." Daffy rolled her eyes. "You were never going to get the slugs out by giving them their least favourite jam!"

"So, you were in on it?" Mucus roared. "I see it all now, as clear as my slime bubbles.

"You were never my friend! And if you're not

my friend, then … you're my *enemy*." He looked from Daffy and Boris, to Fizzbee, to Scooter and Cat. "You're all my enemies!" he screeched as he pressed a button on the remote control and a giant jam jar slowly lowered from the ceiling, a huge dustpan and brush extending out from beside it. "And I know just what to do with my enemies." Mucus rubbed his tentacles together evilly.

CHAPTER ELEVEN

Scooter and Cat tumbled down from the giant dustpan into the enormous jam jar where Daffy, Boris and Fizzbee had already been captured.

"Is everyone OK?" Scooter sat up and dusted himself down, then picked up the little cage that Fizzbee had been padlocked inside.

"Well, I was doing much better before you lot arrived!" Daffy huffed, then gave Boris a tickle under his chin. "Not you of course, Boris."

"Well, that's gratitude!" Cat stood up, then began scouting the giant jam jar for a way out. "Seeing as we were trying to rescue you!" She jumped as she tried to reach the top of the jam jar and slid back down again helplessly. "And what were you doing anyway? Because it looked to me like you were very cosy with the evil slug!"

"I was having a *reasonable conversation* with him!" Daffy bellowed, her eyes practically popping out at the injustice of Cat's remark. "Exactly as we'd planned!" She spoke through her teeth, before turning away and crossing her arms. "It was working a lot better than trying to stink him out with a jam he's *not too keen on*!"

"I really thought the Relaxing Lavender Jam thing would work," Cat sighed as she shoved the slug encyclopedia back into her pocket.

"And anyway, he's not actually *that* evil," Daffy continued witheringly over her shoulder as Cat slumped down next to Scooter. "He's quite nice really. He just wants us to stop seeing him as a garden pest. He wants everyone to know that he's more than that."

"*Really?*" Scooter's eyebrows knitted together as he gave Mucus a long thoughtful look. "I didn't realize that."

"Yes. But he's really cheesed off

with us now. And If I know Mucus, then he'll want revenge." Daffy peered down nervously. "Something *really* creative and stylish, like his dress sense."

They all watched as Mucus wrote two words on the whiteboard below.

"Told you." Daffy tutted. "We're for it now."

Mucus stared at the whiteboard for a moment, then began pacing, his slug slime glowing with a sickly greenish tinge as he muttered and mumbled below them.

"I wish we could hear what he was saying." Cat pressed her ear to the glass.

"Is his slime meant to be that colour?" Scooter's eyes narrowed. "It looks a bit…"

"Toxic!" Fizzbee finished the sentence for him. "Oh, Scooter! That does not look good.

Not good at all. His creativity – it is turning bad! He is having far too many dastardly revenge ideas!"

They watched as Mucus shook his head in frustration, then screeched something.

"I think he said something about needing *more* ideas!" Cat pressed her ear harder against the glass as Mucus slithered over to the vat marked *Cocoa Bean Creativity Jam*.

"No!" Fizzbee cried as Mucus lifted his curly straw towards it. "He must not have any more!"

"Mucus! Don't do it!" Scooter banged on the glass of the jam jar. "It's not good for you!" But Mucus couldn't hear Scooter shouting from inside the jam jar even if he'd wanted to. He dunked the straw into the vat and began slurping it up. The gang could only watch in horror as he swigged and swilled, his slime frothing, foaming and fizzing like a sponge with every gulp.

"What will actually happen if his creativity goes fully toxic?" Cat asked as Mucus's slime turned a fluorescent-green colour, then yellow, then bright pink, then finally the sickly green colour once again.

"He will be filled with so many ideas that his head will explode!" Fizzbee threw her arms around her head to show them what an exploding head might look like. "Fizzbee thought that she had already explained this."

"You mean you were *serious*?" Scooter gasped. "I thought you were joking!"

"Fizzbee does not joke about heads exploding, Scooter." She crossed her arms.

"We can't let his head explode!" Daffy cried. "He's my second-best friend!"

"How can we stop it, Fizz?" Scooter asked urgently.

"Fizzbee does not know, Scooter." Fizzbee shook her head sadly. "Maybe if he could release some of the creativity? But soon he will have so many ideas that making decisions will become impossible, and," she continued matter of factly, "*that* is when his head will explode."

They all peered anxiously at Mucus as he started scrawling ideas onto the whiteboard, all the while barking orders at the Hand-Bots as he wrote.

REVENGE IDEAS

Bounce them all on the jam balloons.
Wrap them in jam wrapping paper.
Stick them to the wall with jam hair gel.
Put them in a packing box.
Dunk them in Brussels Sprout jam.

Scooter sighed. This was not an ideal situation, that was for sure.

They were trapped in a jam jar. The factory was filled with slugs. The Hand-Bots and the machinery were all under the control of Mucus who was filled with toxic creativity and whose head might explode at any second. They had no inventions. No jam. Nothing.

Things really could not get any worse.

DING-DONG.

He turned towards the front door. Was that the doorbell? But who could it be? His heart soared for a moment as he wondered if just maybe his mum and dad had escaped the flat. He wasn't sure they'd be able to help all that much right now, but it would be nice to see their friendly faces at least.

DING-DONG.

The doorbell rang again.

But it wasn't Scooter's parents; it was someone else entirely. And as Scooter watched Mucus open the door to a thin, balding man carrying a clipboard, he realized that things could get much, much worse after all.

The hygiene inspector had come a day early.

"Good morning." A tall, balding man wearing a suit and half-moon spectacles looked up from a clipboard. "I'm Stan Scrubs, the hygiene inspector. Sorry I'm a day early. I…" He paused as he realized that he was talking to a slug. "Oh." His mouth dropped open. "Oh, dear." He tutted as he scribbled something onto his clipboard.

"Hand-Bots!" Mucus shrieked. "Put him in the jam jar with the others!"

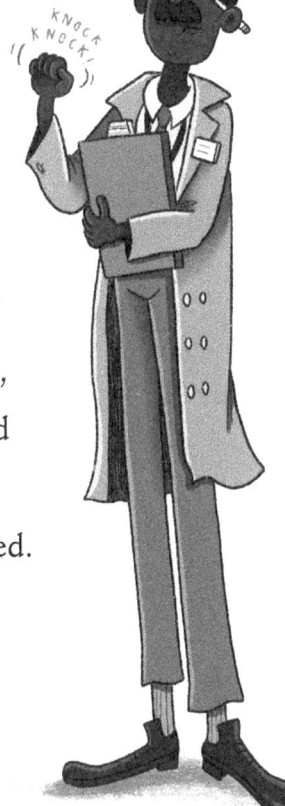

Scooter, Fizzbee, Cat, Daffy, Boris and Stan, the hygiene inspector, sat on the bottom of the jam jar as it hung from the ceiling, watching as Mucus feverishly scribbled more revenge ideas on the whiteboard below, the sickly green slime ballooning, surrounding his little body in a bogey-like bubble as slugs continued to wriggle and writhe their way around the factory.

"This is all Fizzbee's fault." Fizzbee gripped the bars of her little cage, her antennae drooping. "Fizzbee's inventions are *always* going wrong. Fizzbee is useless." She flopped down onto her bottom as a large tear rolled down her face.

"Hey, Fizz, that's not true!" Scooter lifted the little cage up towards him. "Your inventions have saved us loads of times!"

"Not *really*." Fizzbee pulled one antenna over her shoulder. She sniffed as Cat slipped a clip out of her hair and began trying to unpick the padlock of her cage.

"Well, what about that time when Daffy and Boris tried to break in and we trapped Boris inside a giant jam bubble? We couldn't have done that without your Growing Solution." Scooter met her eyes.

"Except that Boris ate it and grew into a giant guinea pig." Daffy studied her fingernails. "It wasn't so good then."

"But remember how much your inventions helped us on our last adventure," Scooter carried on, ignoring Daffy. "We'd never have found Captain DodgyBeard's treasure without your Shrinking Strawberry Jam."

"And we'd never have escaped the vaults without your Anti-Gravity Powder!" Cat added.

"Well, yes..." Daffy pursed her lips. "That's true."

"Squeak." Boris released a heart-shaped poo as the hygiene inspector tutted and wrote something on his clipboard.

"But now Mucus's head is going to explode!" Fizzbee wiped another tear from her face as Cat finally unpicked the padlock and opened the cage door. "And it is all Fizzbee's fault."

"We're not going to let that happen, Fizz." Scooter put the cage down and smiled as Fizzbee toddled out onto his palm. She felt warm and smooth. "And anyway, it's not your fault. It was me thinking that I had to do everything on my own that got us into this." He smiled kindly. "If I'd just let everyone help me with my to-do list, then my creativity would never have become blocked in the first place and Mucus wouldn't have toxic creativity." He hesitated as something sparked inside his mind. Something about what he'd just said. "Wait a minute!" He leapt to his feet. "Of course! We all know how to block Mucus's creativity! After all –" he smiled impishly as the team looked at him blankly – "nothing kills creativity quicker than a long to-do list!"

CHAPTER TWELVE

"I know things seem bad." Scooter gave the hygiene inspector a sheepish glance as he stood in front of his friends with his hands on his hips. "If there's one thing I've learnt today, it's that sometimes things don't go right at first. But as of now, we've got to forget about the factory and focus on how we can save Mucus. Whatever happens, we can't let his head explode." He took a deep breath. "Now, let's stop his toxic creativity. But for my plan to work, we need to get out of this jam jar and release Mucus's control of the Hand-Bots." He looked up at the top of the tall jam jar, then down towards Mucus, who was feverishly scrawling more ideas on the whiteboard, the bubble of toxic creativity growing bigger with every passing moment. "And we need to do it fast," he added.

"Well, I could have stood in front of everyone and said *that*!" Daffy huffed. "But *how*?"

Scooter didn't reply as he concentrated on reaching into his pocket. It was tricky and he had to be careful, but finally he pulled out a slightly crumbly jam tart. He passed it down to Fizzbee, smiling as she pattered onto it and hovered up in front of his face. "Fizzbee, if we create a distraction, do you think that you can get to the remote control?"

"Fizzbee can try." Fizzbee nodded. "But, Scooter?" she peered down nervously at Mucus. "What if Mucus sees Fizzbee? The Hand-Bots are very big. And they have already caught Fizzbee once."

"Don't worry about that." Scooter shook his head. "We'll distract Mucus so that he doesn't notice you. Once you've got the remote control, just take out the batteries and the Hand-Bots will respond to my voice commands again and as soon as we've got the hand-bots back – " Scooter grinned – "then I know what to do."

"But how are we going to distract Mucus?" Cat tapped on the glass of the jar. "He can't hear us from in here, remember?"

"That's actually the trickiest part of my plan." Scooter took a deep breath. "We're going to have to work together." He looked from Daffy, to Boris, to Cat, to Stan, the hygiene inspector, as the team huddled together. "And I mean, *all* of us." He raised his eyebrows. "OK, here's the plan."

Mucus scribbled on the whiteboard furiously as revenge plots and plans and ploys whizzed frantically around inside his brain.

Spray them with plant spray.

Catapult them out of the factory.

Blast them with hot air.

"So many ideas!" He gave his head a shake, the pressure building inside him. "But which one is best?"

Lick their noses.

Fling them out of the front door!

Give them a rollercoaster ride they'll NEVER FORGET.

"Too – many – ideas!" he wailed as the giant glimmering snot bubble started to wibble and wobble, quivering and quavering as it grew and grew, surrounding him in a ball of green light until, like a slug-shaped slimy glitter ball, he rose into the air.

"Coooo-eeeeeee... Mucus?" He looked up towards the jam jar to see Daffy's head poking out from above the rim.

"Daffy?" He squinted up in confusion. Was Daffy at the top of a human (and guinea pig) triangle? Yes! She was standing shakily on the shoulders of the health inspector and the girl, as her supposed *best friend*, Boris, held up one lace of her shoe and Scooter directed them to one side.

"There's a lot to do to maintain a factory, I mean, ahem, a slug café and wellness spa." Daffy pointed up to the ceiling innocently. "Like getting the jars of Floating Fig Jam down from the ceiling."

"What?" Mucus looked up towards the ceiling, momentarily distracted from his dastardly plans.

"And –" Daffy bent down to listen to Scooter from the bottom of the jar before poking her head back up – "there's also looking after all of the plants. And oiling the rollercoaster. And umm ... making jam."

"I ... well ... I..." Mucus hesitated, his mind completely blank.

Pffffffff.

A tiny bubble of air escaped from the slime bubble of toxic creativity.

"Oi!" He shook his head. "What are you doing?"

Scooter watched from the jam jar as Fizzbee hovered cautiously towards Mucus and the remote control.

"Are you sure this is the best way to distract him?" Daffy asked out of the corner of her mouth. "Because I think he might have figured out that we're up to something?"

"Just keep going!" Scooter whispered back as Fizzbee hid behind the vat of jam hair gel, just metres away from the remote control. "I think it's actually working. Did you see his creativity bubble pop a little bit then? Keep listing boring jobs. We need to keep him distracted long enough for Fizzbee to get to the remote control."

"Hopefully, that won't be too long." Cat wheezed from below Daffy. "I have to say, I can't help wondering why Daffy's at the top of this human triangle."

"Because I'm Mucus's best friend." Daffy hissed from above. "Now please keep me steady." She poked her head over the rim of the jar. "Mucus? Have you noticed the windows need a clean? And there's an awful lot of slime around the place." She looked around the factory. "Actually, never mind the windows, I think the whole place needs a clean. The floor ... the walls ... the plants ... the conveyor belts..."

"Stop that!" Mucus shook his head, as another *pfffft* of air escaped his creativity bubble and he lowered slightly to the ground.

"My armpits..." Daffy continued as she gave her armpits a sniff. "The bog..."

"And Boris ... he stinks." Cat added. "I'll be giving you a bath myself after we're out of here, your fur reeks of mouldy Brussels sprouts." She wrinkled her nose as Boris rolled his eyes and plonked himself down on her shoulder with a weary sigh.

Stan, the hygiene inspector, gave an approving nod and added a little tick to his clipboard on the other side of the human triangle.

"NOW, FIZZBEE!" Scooter yelled even though he knew she couldn't hear him, as Fizzbee dived towards the remote control.

"Oi!" Mucus cried as Fizzbee snatched it out of his sensory tentacles, yanked open the back and emptied it of batteries. "OI!" he roared again.

But it was too late. As soon as the batteries were out of

the remote control, the Hand-Bots were no longer under his power.

"You'll regret that!" Mucus bellowed as he turned back to the whiteboard, his sickly green creativity bubble blooming and blossoming with fresh revenge ideas.

"His head!" Daffy wailed. "It's gonna blow!"

But Scooter knew exactly what to do. With a short whistle, the Hand-Bots were by his side once more.

"Hand-Bots –" he raised his eyebrows – "please can you show Mucus the to-do list?"

"What?" Mucus scoffed.

"How is that going to...?" He stared open-mouthed as Hand-Bot Two pulled out a scroll and unfurled it to the ground with a flourish.

It unravelled and rolled around Mucus, his eyes growing wide at the endless list of jobs.

"Nooooooooooooooooooooo!" he wailed as the giant glimmering bogey bubble of toxic creativity began to convulse and vibrate.

Pffftttt. Pfffftttt. PFFFFFFTTTTTtt.

Wafts of green smoke began to escape and they watched as the slime turned from the yucky shade of vomit green, to blue, to pink, to yellow, until Mucus was surrounded in a beautiful slime ball of colours and light.

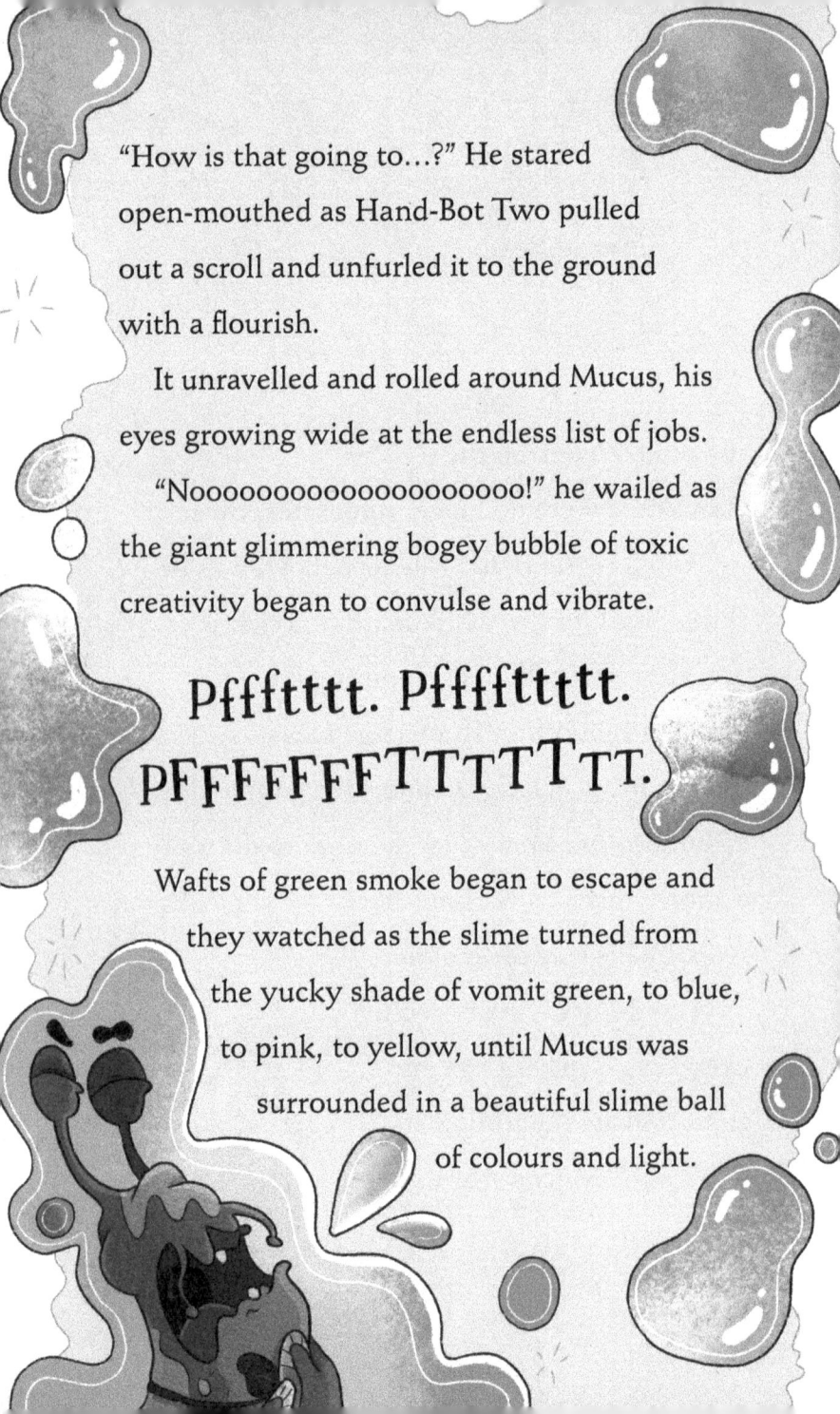

"Fizzbee? What's happening?" Scooter gasped. "Is he all right?"

"Yes, Scooter. It is OK," Fizzbee reassured him. "The toxic creativity has dispersed. What you see now is *pure* creativity."

"Oh!" Scooter stared in amazement. "Wow! Is this what creativity looks like to you, Fizz?"

"Yes, Scooter." Fizzbee smiled. "Except a bit less…"

SQUEEEELLLLLLLCCCCHHHHHHHHH!

The creativity slime bubble exploded like a giant gooey firework into the factory.

"Squelchy." Fizzbee finished her sentence as colourful, sticky slime rained down on them.

"Urgh." Scooter put his arm over his head. "Slug slime rain. Gross."

"Enough!" Mucus's little brown body slumped back down to the ground in defeat. "I don't care if I never have another idea in my whole life!"

"Wait a minute! He can still talk!" Cat cried as the Hand-Bots carefully lowered the giant jam jar from the ceiling, releasing Scooter and the team into the factory. "Does that mean…?"

"No, it is OK." Fizzbee studied Mucus as he curled up on the floor. "He is just an everyday talking garden slug now. There is nothing special about him."

"Actually, there is." Daffy picked him up carefully. "He's special because he's my second-best friend and he's very clever."

"Really, Daffy?" Mucus looked up from the palm of her hand.

"Yes, of course!" Daffy smiled down at him fondly. "I loved chatting with you earlier. But that Cocoa Bean Creativity Jam was giving you far too many dastardly ideas."

"Yes, it was a bit, wasn't it?" Mucus snotted out a sheepish little slime bubble.

"Squeak." Boris nodded in agreement.

"Ahem." A cough behind made them all turn in surprise to where Stan, the hygiene inspector stood politely waiting. He was covered head to toe in green slug slime.

"Oh." Scooter's face fell. "I forgot about you."

"Yeeeeees." He held up his clipboard.

Willowden Council

WILLOWDEN GREEN BRANCH

Hygiene Inspection of McLay's Jam Factory

OVERALL RESULT FAIL

Cleanliness of Overall Factory:
TERRIBLE!
The whole place is covered in slug slime
[X] ☹

Cleanliness of Equipment:
DISGUSTING!
Everything was covered in SLUGS!
[X] ☹

Jam Hygiene:
DREADFUL!
Slugs swimming in the jam.
[X] ☹

Summary:
FAIL!! - McLay's jam factory is currently falling a long way below the hygiene standards expected from a jam factory of its reputation!

Recommendation: IMMEDIATE CLOSURE!!!

"I'm afraid that you've failed the hygiene inspection." Stan wiped the slime off his half-moon spectacles. "And as such this factory should be closed right now."

CHAPTER THIRTEEN

Scooter stared at the clipboard in front of him. There was no doubt about it. They might have saved Mucus but they'd failed in everything else.

The whole factory was drenched in slime. Slugs wriggled and writhed everywhere. There was even a slug by his feet, nibbling at his shoe.

He sighed. Stan was right. The place was disgusting.

"But –" Stan lifted the top sheet to reveal a second sheet below – "it wasn't *all* bad."

> Standards:
> NOT TOO BAD! There was an impressive to-do list and a guinea pig wearing a HAZMAT suit, suggesting that Standards are normally higher than observed.
>
> Leadership: GOOD!
> Scooter McLay seems like a respected and worthy leader!

"I have to admit that I was impressed by your leadership, Scooter." Stan carefully removed a little slug from his clipboard as it nibbled on the report. "It's a shame, really." He put the clipboard under his arm. "I've always loved McLay's jam. Cherry Candyfloss is my absolute favourite. If only I'd come a day or two late rather than a day early." He sighed.

"But wait!" Fizzbee hovered in front of him in her jam tart. "If it had not been for Scooter, then this poor slug would have lost his life. His head was about to explode!" She turned towards Mucus expectantly.

Mucus hesitated as he met her eyes, then shrugged.

"It's true." He raised his eyebrows. "This boy saved my life. Having said that, I was about to launch my brand-new jam flavour idea, which I must add was vastly superior to any of his."

"Exactly!" Cat agreed, then frowned. "About the saving-his-life bit, I mean. Not the jam bit. But anyway, I think we can all agree that Scooter's a hero! Surely he deserves another chance?"

"And seeing as you're a day early, I don't think this hygiene inspection really counts." Daffy gave Stan a stony look. "Can't you just come back in a day or two?"

"**Squeak**." Boris nodded from inside his hazmat suit.

The hygiene inspector took a deep breath as he gave each member of the team a long look. Slowly and carefully, he took the paper from the clipboard.

"I've decided not to submit this report." He tore the pages to pieces and dropped them to the floor. "I liked what you said earlier, Scooter, about things not always being right at first. Perhaps that can apply today." He raised his eyebrows. "I will return in three days, when I will conduct a new inspection."

"You mean if we clear up the factory before then, we won't be closed down?" Scooter asked, his eyes full of hope.

"That's right." The hygiene inspector nodded. "But I have to warn you, there will be no third chances." He took off his shoe and emptied it of slime, before slipping it back on and squelching his way towards the door. "See you in three days," he added without a backwards glance.

Scooter turned to look at his friends, his grin wide. OK, so the factory was in ruins, and he had no idea how they were going to clean it up in time, but he knew that if they all worked together, then they could do it.

"One challenge at a time, Scooter." Fizzbee hovered up towards him. "And the next challenge is to get the slugs out."

"You're right." Scooter nodded. "And I've had an idea about that." He turned to Mucus. "What would you say if I offered you a job?"

"A job?" Mucus replied warily. "What kind of job?"

"I'm looking for a new Compost Heap Manager," Scooter continued importantly. "Someone smart and resourceful. Someone who can organize slugs. Someone who likes rotten vegetables." He smiled. "Would you be interested?"

"Hmm." Mucus preened his bow tie with

his sensory tentacle. "I'll consider it. But what about my slug café and wellness spa? I had such great plans."

"Oh, Mucus, the compost heap would be the perfect place for it!" Daffy beamed. "It would be full of lovely rotten fruit and vegetables and it would be free of your predators!"

"That does sound *quite* nice." The corners of Mucus's lip twitched. "I'll have to think about it."

"Fair enough." Scooter turned towards the little slug still sliming on his shoe. "I wonder if there are any other slugs who would like to apply."

"What?" Mucus cried. "No ordinary slug could do a job as important as Compost Heap Manager. No, it's OK, I've had a think and I'll take the job!"

"Brilliant." Scooter grinned. "Well, your first task is to get all of the slugs into the compost heap."

"Well, that's easy." Mucus thrust his chest out importantly. "Hand-Bots!" he ordered. "Open the compost chute!" The Hand-Bots remained where they were beside Scooter. "Oh, whoops." Mucus cleared his throat sheepishly. "Old habits and all that. Scooter, if *you* wouldn't mind asking the Hand-Bots to open the compost chute." He lifted a loudspeaker. "Then I'll get the slugs down there in five minutes' flat." Scooter gave the Hand-Bots a nod to open the compost chute and Daffy placed Mucus carefully at the top of it. Mucus lifted the megaphone to his rear end and …

SQUEELLLLLLLCCCCHHHHHH SQUISSSSSSHHHHHHHHHH! he snotted out through the loudspeaker.

All of the slugs stopped what they were doing immediately and began slithering their way towards him.

"Tally-ho, gang!" Mucus winked as he threw himself down the chute into the tunnel followed by hundreds, no thousands, of little slugs. "Wheeeeeeeeeeeeeeeeeeeeee!" they heard him squeal in delight as he slid down into the compost heap.

"Right, everyone." Scooter marched to the front of the whiteboard as Hand-Bot One extended loyally beside him carrying a pen. "There's a lot of work to do to get the factory ready for the hygiene inspection." He stared at the ruins around them. "Let's make a plan…" He paused. "But first … we should probably help my mum and dad get out of the flat."

CHAPTER FOURTEEN

The next two days were spent in a flurry of activity as Scooter's to-do list was split between the team.

Daffy, Boris and Mucus worked together on the compost heap, turning it into the best-ever slug café and wellness spa. They built a mouldy vegetable juice swimming pool, banana peel slumber pods, even fungal face masks. And, of course, a rotten cabbage juice bar.

Cat tended the poor plants that had been eaten by the slugs. She removed the rotten leaves, replanted Brussels sprouts to maintain power and dotted lavender plants around the factory to deter slugs from coming back inside.

Scooter's mum and dad took out their mops and scrubbing brushes and gave the factory a deep clean.

Scooter oversaw the giant robotic tools and machinery as all of the contaminated jam was drained out of the factory, while Fizzbee worked quietly on a new invention of her own.

A new *secret* invention that she said would help them.

Two days later and the factory gleamed and sparkled whilst the slugs were happy in their new home.

There was just one thing. Scooter hadn't liked to mention it to the team while they were all working so hard but there was actually still a *huge* problem.

The factory might be clean enough to pass a hygiene inspection, but the waterfalls were switched off. The jam rivers were empty. The conveyor belts were still and quiet. There were no strawberries on the strawberry wall. No blueberries on the hedgerows. Not one watermelon or cocoa bean in sight. The plants might have survived the slug invasion, but it would be some months before they were recovered enough to grow fruit again.

And no fruit meant no *jam.*

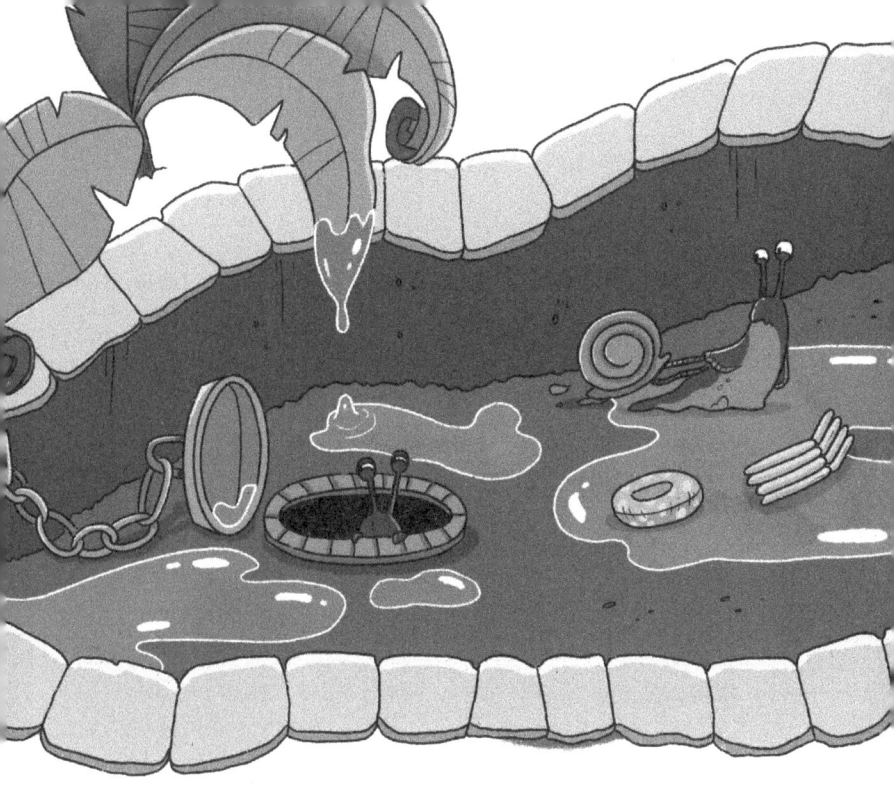

Even if they passed the hygiene inspection, McLay's jam factory would have to temporarily close.

"It won't be for too long, Scoot." Cat put her hand on his shoulder after he'd explained the situation to the team as they all stood staring at the sterile, empty factory. "Well, only six months or so, I mean."

"Six months?" Scooter sighed. He hadn't realized it would take that long.

"Yeah." Cat nodded sadly. "And that's only if we *really* look after the plants."

"Scooter?" Fizzbee hovered over from her workbench, a little sprayer in her hand. "Fizzbee has something that can help."

Everyone paused to look at Fizzbee as she lifted a little spray bottle, labelled Rotten Cabbage Fertilizer Jam, with a nervous smile.

"Fizzbee has been working verrrrrry carefully on this invention." She fluttered down to one of Cat's seedling trays. She lifted a small seedling plant, gave it the tiniest of sprays and Scooter gasped as the little plant immediately thrust out two new leaves and grew two inches.

Scooter hesitated.

Maybe using Fizzbee's invention to solve their problems wasn't the right thing. After all, trying to magically fix his problems hadn't worked so well recently.

"Fizzbee should never have created the Cocoa Bean Creativity Jam." Fizzbee met Scooter's uncertain gaze. "Creativity jam wasn't solving a problem, it was covering up a problem. But Fizzbee's fertilizer is not like that; it will help the plants grow strong and healthy.

Fizzbee has tested and tested and Fizzbee is sure that there are no side effects. Except –" she hesitated – "it will take a month for the plants to grow fruit again. Any quicker and the mixture would be unstable." She bit her lip and looked to the floor before mumbling, "That is if Scooter still trusts Fizzbee's inventions."

"Oh, Fizz, of course I still trust your inventions!" Scooter put his hand out and smiled as Fizzbee landed on it. "But Cat's in charge of plant care now." He turned towards Cat as she picked up the little seedling and studied it carefully. "So, she gets to decide."

"I think it could definitely work." Cat looked up with a grin. "Plus, in the month that the factory is closed while we wait for the plants to grow, you can have a proper break, Scooter. We could all have a holiday and some fun."

"That actually sounds really nice." Scooter beamed.

"It's good to see you working as a team." Scooter's mum put her hand on his shoulder. "I can't believe you didn't talk to us about your enormous to-do list. You don't need to do everything alone, you know."

"I do know." Scooter nodded as he looked at the smiling faces surrounding him. "I've got the best team ever to help me."

DING-DONG.

They all turned towards the front door as Stan, the Hygiene Inspector, stood outside with his clipboard.

"Good morning." He beamed as he pushed his half-moon spectacles onto his nose and looked around the factory with an approving smile. "I see you've been busy!"

CHAPTER FIFTEEN

One month later...

"Ready?" Scooter grinned as Fizzbee, Cat, Daffy, Boris, Mum and Dad stood beside him.

"Ready!" they all chorused back.

He lifted his hand towards a giant *ON* button and pressed it.

CHUGGA, CHUGGA, CHUGGA, WHOOOOOOSSSSHHHH!

Almost at once, the jam waterfalls began spilling down from the ceiling and the wonderful smell of fresh fruit and sugar wafted towards them as the jam streams and brooks began to flow and frolic around the factory.

The conveyor belt started chugging along, jam jars tinkling merrily as giant robotic squirters plopped jam into the jam jars. The Banana Jam Bubble Bath began bubbling, the Jam Wrapping Paper began rolling and everything began to trundle and tumble along exactly as it should.

"Well done, son." Mum stood beside Scooter as they both looked at the Hygiene Inspection Gold Star Award hanging on the wall. "It's almost like the slugs were never here!"

"Except for the compost heap, that is." Scooter smiled as he looked at the new press cutting on the wall beside it.

SLUG TAKES JOB AT McLAY'S JAM FACTORY

Mucus Vane, a genius talking slug, has become the latest addition to the McLay's jam factory team, managing the compost heap on behalf of Chief Inventor, Scooter McLay.

"Mucus was the obvious choice for the job," Scooter told us exclusively. "He's even turned the compost heap into a brand-new slug café and wellness spa."

Unfortunately, the slug spa has a strict slug-and-best-friends-only entry policy. However, an inside source says their skin has never looked so good.

This reporter, for one, will be looking at slugs in a whole new light from now on.

Below it was a picture of Mucus sitting on a sun-lounger drinking a rotten cabbage juice from a curly straw, looking smug.

"Only you could turn a problem into a solution." Dad ruffled his hair. "We're really proud of you, Scoot."

Scooter smiled as he listened to the comforting sound of the factory. He'd missed its constant whirr and whizz and whoosh over the last month, though he had to admit he'd had a brilliant time doing all the things he loved. Riding daily on the rollercoaster. Competing in jam ball tournaments, using up all the old slug-infested jam. Developing a brand-new jam flume ride on the jam rivers and, of course, testing it thoroughly. Not to mention all of the time he'd spent with Fizzbee coming up with new jam inventions in his jam inventions book:

IDEAS (BY SCOOTER & FIZZBEE)

- JAM-FILLED PIÑATA
- BOUNCY JAM SHOES
- INVISIBILITY JAM
- JAM FOAM PARTY!

Scooter's creativity block was well and truly *unblocked* and his ideas were feeling really very whizzy and whoossshy and zippy and sparky again.

"We're off to see Mucus." Daffy and Boris drove in on her patrol buggy with a bottle of rotten cabbage juice and a bag of Brussels sprouts. "It's time for my daily slug slime facial."

"Actually –" Scooter grinned as a little slug wearing a hazmat suit waved to them from the top of the compost chute – "I've invited Mucus into the factory today. I thought that we could all celebrate together with a little party, and Fizzbee and I could show you some of our new inventions."

He watched happily as the Hand-Bots tied a jam piñata to the ceiling, then began laying tables with Jam Fizz, Jam Party plates, lots of delicious food and, of course, plenty of rotten cabbage juice for Mucus. He closed his jam inventions book and gave Fizzbee a wink, then lifted a remote control and pressed a new button. There was a **WHOOOSH** and a whirrrrr and the rivers and streams began to fizz and froth until clouds of delicious-smelling jam foam floated into the air around them. "Edible jam clouds!" he laughed as Fizzbee launched into the air, her mouth open wide. "And that's not all." He handed out butterfly nets so that everyone could catch themselves a jam cloud, then pressed another button on the remote control and smiled as a large jam jar boat bounced towards them along the foaming river. "How about some jam water rafting?" He gazed up at the jam waterfall stretching above them. "The Fall of Foam has increased the thrill factor by 107.11%." Scooter gave his friends a cheeky wink. "So, who wants a ride?"

What is Cerebral palsy?

The hero of this book, Scooter McLay, has cerebral palsy. This is a condition that affects his movement and muscle control. The messages between his brain and his body can get a little jumbled or lost.

Cerebral → brain
Palsy → difficulty with controlling muscles, and therefore movement, in the body

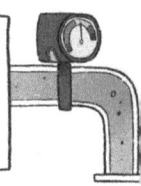

Cerebral palsy can affect different parts of the body.

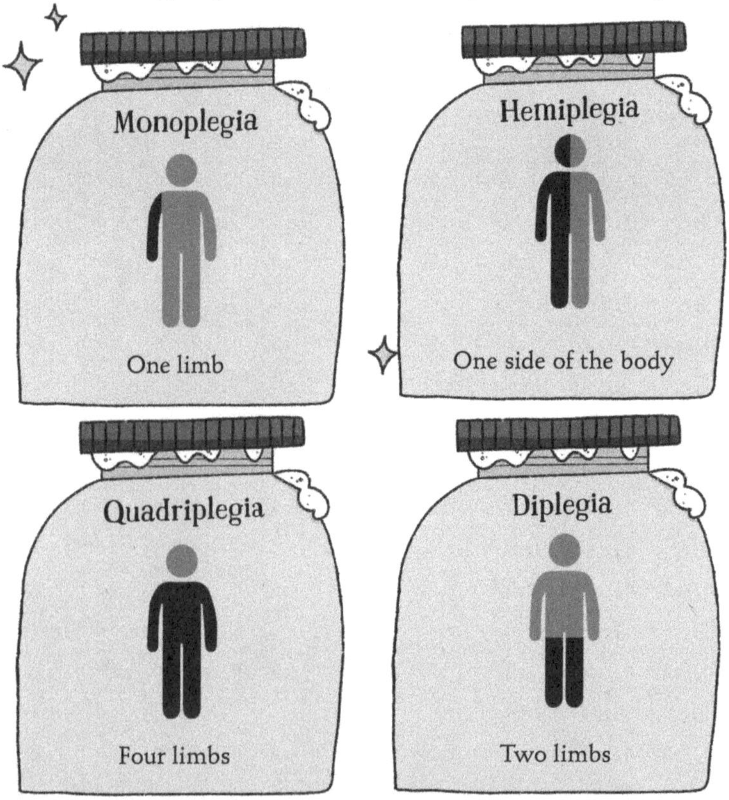

Monoplegia	Hemiplegia
One limb	One side of the body

Quadriplegia	Diplegia
Four limbs	Two limbs

For Scooter, it means that the muscles on the left side of his body are a little stiff and he wears a splint on his left leg to give him extra support to allow him to stand and walk more easily. However, cerebral palsy affects every person differently.

Cerebral palsy affects around 1 in 400 children born in the UK

These are the main types of cerebral palsy:

- **Spastic cerebral palsy**
  This is the most common type. Spasticity makes the muscles tight and stiff, reducing movement.

- **Dyskinetic (athetoid) cerebral palsy**
  Dyskinetic cerebral palsy causes uncontrolled body movements and can affect speech or language.

- **Ataxic cerebral palsy**
  Ataxia makes balance and co-ordination difficult, leading to shaky movements. This can affect speech and language.

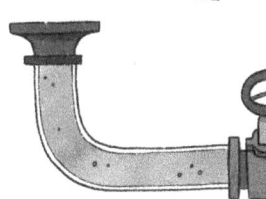

People with CP have it all their lives

Cerebral palsy can cause problems with movement, breathing, balance, sleeping, eating, posture, hearing, sight and communication

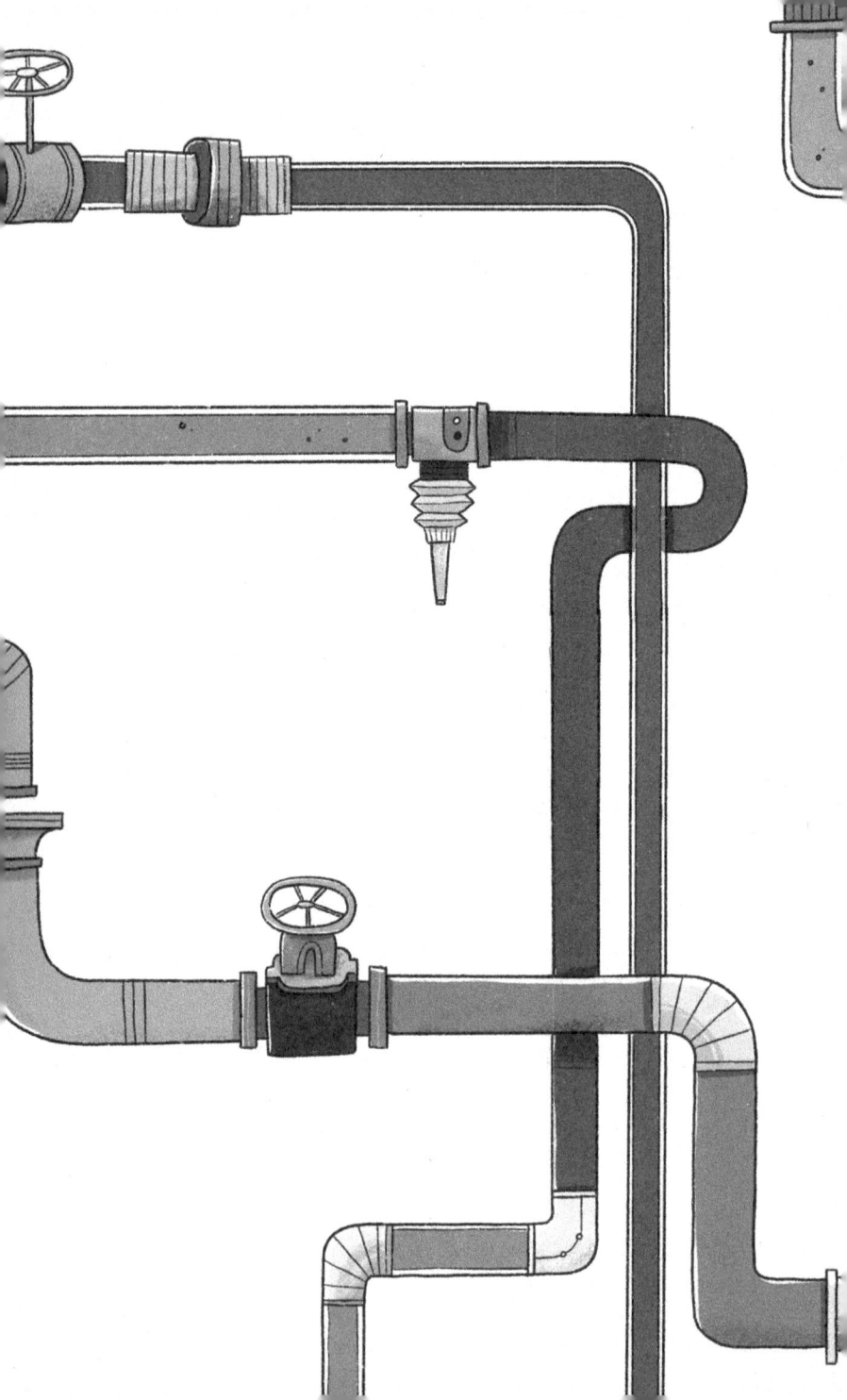

Acknowledgements

When I first started writing this book, I thought that I might come to like slugs a bit more. That didn't happen (sorry, slugs). But I have learnt a lot about the pesky little blighters and especially their slug slime. Slugs need their slime for everything – sticking to walls, communicating, even protection! They simply couldn't manage without it ... just like I couldn't manage without the incredible team of professionals, friends and family who support me. So, while I appreciate that being likened to slug slime might not seem very flattering, I mean it as the highest of compliments when I say that the following people are the slime to this slug.

Thank you so much (or Gloopy Poopy Pfffft in Slimeish) to:

- My brilliant agent, Kate Shaw.
- My Editor, Frances Taffinder – I love working with you and I'm so grateful for your unwavering support and expert guidance.
- Jamie Hammond – Best (and loveliest) Designer EVER.
- The whole wonderful team at Walker Books and especially PR legends, Rebecca Oram and Niabh Rowland Simms – thank you for all that you do.

- Jenny Taylor – for bringing the jam factory and all who dwell there to life. Also, for always jumping on board with my schemes, even when it means washing slime out of your hair for days afterwards.
- My amazing Golden Egg buddies and creative hive mind; George, Cathie, Adam, Elizabeth, Jenny, Georgia, John, Sarah, Amy & Alex. Special mentions to Kate Perry, for her amazing brainstorm sessions, unwavering cheerleading, and her patient beta reading. And to Kerry Mintern, for coming up with the brilliant slug name, Mucus Vane. #Moraleishigh.
- My fellow writers on Twitter and Instagram and especially Annaliese Avery, for all of her invaluable support and much-needed pep talks.
- All of the booksellers, bloggers, reviewers and educators and readers who have championed the Jam Factory – I wouldn't be here without you.
- My friends & family – Mum, Dad, Colin, Anne, Matt, Helen, Thomas, Isaac, Jona, Marie-Lou, Evie, Oliver, Dave, Stacey, Faithe & Jax. You are all brilliant.
- All of my lovely friends and especially Smallie, Joshie, Lucy, Rob, Albert, Edith, Michelle, Lindsay & Laura.
- Abigail, my goddaughter, who continues to inspire Scooter's adventures and her mum, Carrie, my super special friend and our sensitivity reader.
- And finally, my wonderful husband, Richie and our two children, Meg and Hattie, who always believe in me and offer a constant supply of ideas, giggles and hugs.